John Hay, Henry Morley

Pike County Ballads

John Hay, Henry Morley

Pike County Ballads

ISBN/EAN: 9783742899774

Manufactured in Europe, USA, Canada, Australia, Japa

Cover: Foto ©Andreas Hilbeck / pixelio.de

Manufactured and distributed by brebook publishing software (www.brebook.com)

John Hay, Henry Morley

Pike County Ballads

PIKE COUNTY BALLADS

AND OTHER POEMS

BY

COLONEL JOHN HAY

EDITED, WITH AN INTRODUCTION, BY

HENRY MORLEY, LL.D.

EMERITUS PROFESSOR OF ENGLISH LANGUAGE AND
LITERATURE AT UNIVERSITY COLLEGE
LONDON

LONDON
GEORGE ROUTLEDGE & SONS, LIMITED
BROADWAY, LUDGATE HILL
MANCHESTER AND NEW YORK
1897

CONTENTS.

INTRODUCTION.

PIKE COUNTY BALLADS and other poems in this
volume by Colonel John Hay represent in the
best manner the spirit of our strong and independent sister-land across the Atlantic. Pike County
Ballads do full justice to the raw material in the
United States, and show a loyal temper in the
rough. The other pieces show how the love of
freedom speaks through finer spirits of the land,
and, dealing with realities, can turn a life of action
into music.

Colonel Hay has lived always in vigorous rela-
tion with the full life of the people whose best
mind his poems represent. He is descended from
a Scottish soldier, a John Hay, who, at the beginning of the last century, left his country to take
service under the Elector-Palatine, and whose son
went afterwards with his family to settle among
the Kentucky pioneers. Dr. Charles Hay was the
father of John Hay the poet, who was born on the
8th of October 1838, in the heart of the United
States, at Salem in Indiana. When twenty years
old he graduated at the neighbouring Brown University, where his fellow-students valued his skill
as a writer. Then he studied for the Bar, and he
was called to the Bar three years later, at Springfield, Illinois.

At Springfield, Abraham Lincoln practised as
a barrister. Shrewd, lively, earnest, honest, he
grudged help to a rogue. In a criminal case, when

evidence threw unexpected light upon a client's character, Abraham Lincoln said suddenly to his junior, " Swett, the man is guilty ; you defend him, I can't." In another case, when a piece of rascality in his client came out, Abraham Lincoln left his junior in possession of the case and went to his hotel. To the judge, who sent for him, he replied that he had found his hands were very dirty, and had gone away to get them clean. Almost immediately after John Hay's call to the Bar at Springfield he was chosen by Abraham Lincoln, newly made President, to go with him to Washington. At Washington, Hay acted as Assistant-Secretary, and was also, in the Civil War, *aide-de-camp* to President Lincoln. Throughout that momentous struggle he was actively employed on the side of the North at the headquarters and on the field of battle. He served for a time under Generals Hunter and Gillmore, became a Colonel in the army of the North, and served also as Assistant Adjutant-General. John Hay had in that struggle three brothers and two brothers-in-law serving also in the field.

In 1890 there was published, in ten volumes, at New York, by the New York Century Company, " Abraham Lincoln, a History : by John G. Nicolay and John Hay." This was, with fresh material inserted, a collection of chapters that had been published in *The Century Magazine* from November 1886 to the beginning of 1890. The friends, who worked equally together upon this large record, said, " We knew Mr. Lincoln intimately before his election to the Presidency. We came from Illinois to Washington with him, and remained at his side and in his service—separately or together—until the day of his death."

Abroad, as at home, Colonel Hay has been active in the service of his country. In 1865 he went to Paris as Secretary of Legation, and after remaining two years in that office he went as *Chargé-d'Affaires* for the United States to Vienna. After a year at

Vienna, Colonel Hay went to Madrid as Secretary of Legation under General Daniel Sickles. In 1870 he returned to the United States, and was for the next five years an editorial writer for the New York *Tribune*. During seven months, when White-law Reid was in Europe, Colonel Hay was editor in chief.

It was for *The Tribune* that Hay wrote "The Pike County Ballads," which were first reprinted separately in 1871, and are placed first in the collection of his poems. In the same year he published his "Castilian Days," inspired by residence in Spain.

In 1876 Colonel Hay removed from New York to Cleveland, Ohio. He then ceased to take part in the editing of *The Tribune*, but continued friendly service as a writer. From 1879 to 1881 Colonel Hay served under President Hayes as Assistant-Secretary of State in the Government of the United States. In 1881 he was President of the International Sanitary Congress at Washington. Since that time he has been active, with John G. Nicolay, in the preparation and production of the full Memoir of Abraham Lincoln, now completed, that will take high rank among the records of a war which, in its issues, touched the future of the world, perhaps, more nearly than any war since Waterloo, not even excepting the great struggle which ended at Sedan.

That is the life of a man, here is its music.

Since there is room in this volume for more verses than Colonel Hay's, I have added to them a few poems by Sir Walter Scott ; the first written in 1811 at the time of the struggle with Napoleon in the Peninsula, the second in 1815, after Waterloo. Thus there is over all this volume a thin haze of battle through which we see only the finer feelings and the nobler hopes of man. The day is to come when war shall be no more, but wars have been and may again be necessary to bring on that day ;

A 2

and it is of such war, not untinged with the light
of heaven, that we have passing shadows in this
little book.

"The Vision of Don Roderick; a Poem, by
Walter Scott, Esq.," was printed at Edinburgh by
James Ballantyne & Co. in 1811. They are the
present representatives of that firm by whom it is
here reprinted. It was originally inscribed "to
John Whitmore, Esq., and to the Committee of
Subscribers for relief of the Portuguese Sufferers,
in which he presides," as a "poem composed for
the benefit of the Fund under their management."

The Legend of Don Roderick will be given in
the next volume of our "Companion Poets," for
Robert Southey founded upon it a Romantic Tale
in Verse, which is one of the best tales of the kind in
the English language. Southey's tale of Roderick
himself was written at the same time when Walter
Savage Landor was writing a play upon the sub-
ject, and Scott was, in the piece here reprinted,
making it the starting-point of a vision of the war
in the Peninsula. The fatal palace of Don Roderick may have been a fable connected with the
ruins of a Roman amphitheatre. The fable, as
translated by Scott from a Spanish History of
King Roderick, was this :—

"One mile on the east side of the city of Toledo,
among some rocks, was situated an ancient Tower
of magnificent structure, though much dilapidated
by time, which consumes all : four estadoes (*i.e.*,
four times a man's height) below it, there was a
Cave with a very narrow entrance, and a gate cut
out of the solid rock, lined with a strong covering
of iron, and fastened with many locks ; above
the gate some Greek letters are engraved, which,
although abbreviated, and of doubtful meaning,
were thus interpreted, according to the exposition
of learned men :—The King who opens this cave
and discovers the wonders will discover both good
and evil things. Many kings desired to know the
mystery of this Tower, and sought to find out the

manner with much care; but when they opened
the gate, such a tremendous noise arose in the
Cave that it appeared as if the earth was bursting;
many of those present sickened with fear, and
others lost their lives. In order to prevent such
great perils (as they supposed a dangerous en-
chantment was contained within), they secured the
gate with new locks, concluding, that though a
king was destined to open it, the fated time was
not yet arrived. At last King Don Rodrigo, led
on by his evil fortune and unlucky destiny, opened
the Tower; and some bold attendants whom he
had brought with him entered, although agitated
with fear. Having proceeded a good way, they
fled back to the entrance, terrified with a frightful
vision which they had beheld. The King was
greatly moved, and ordered many torches, so
contrived that the tempest in the cave could not
extinguish them, to be lighted. Then the King
entered, not without fear, before all the others.
He discovered, by degrees, a splendid hall, ap-
parently built in a very sumptuous manner; in the
middle stood a Bronze Statue of very ferocious
appearance, which held a battle-axe in its hands.
With this he struck the floor violently, giving it
such heavy blows that the noise in the Cave was
occasioned by the motion of the air. The King,
greatly affrighted and astonished, began to con-
jure this terrible vision, promising that he would
return without doing any injury in the Cave, after
he had obtained sight of what was contained in
it. The Statue ceased to strike the floor, and the
King, with his followers, somewhat assured, and
recovering their courage, proceeded into the hall;
and on the left of the Statue they found this in-
scription on the wall: 𝕌𝔫𝔣𝔬𝔯𝔱𝔲𝔫𝔞𝔱𝔢 𝕶𝔦𝔫𝔤, 𝔱𝔥𝔬𝔲 𝔥𝔞𝔰𝔱
𝔢𝔫𝔱𝔢𝔯𝔢𝔡 𝔥𝔢𝔯𝔢 𝔦𝔫 𝔞𝔫 𝔢𝔳𝔦𝔩 𝔥𝔬𝔲𝔯. On the right side
of the wall the words were inscribed: 𝕭𝔶 𝔰𝔱𝔯𝔞𝔫𝔤𝔢
𝕹𝔞𝔱𝔦𝔬𝔫𝔰 𝔱𝔥𝔬𝔲 𝔰𝔥𝔞𝔩𝔱 𝔟𝔢 𝔡𝔦𝔰𝔭𝔬𝔰𝔰𝔢𝔰𝔰𝔢𝔡, 𝔞𝔫𝔡 𝔱𝔥𝔶 𝔰𝔲𝔟𝔧𝔢𝔠𝔱𝔰
𝔣𝔬𝔲𝔩𝔩𝔶 𝔡𝔢𝔤𝔯𝔞𝔡𝔢𝔡. On the shoulders of the Statue
other words were written, which said, 𝔍 𝔠𝔞𝔩𝔩 𝔲𝔭𝔬𝔫

the Arabs. And upon his heart was written, *I do my office*. At the entrance of the hall there was placed a round bowl, from which a great noise, like the fall of waters, proceeded. They found no other thing in the hall,—and when the King, sorrowful and greatly affected, had scarcely turned about to leave the Cavern, the Statue again commenced its accustomed blows upon the floor. After they had mutually promised to conceal what they had seen, they again closed the Tower, and blocked up the gate of the Cavern with earth, that no memory might remain in the world of such a portentous and evil-boding prodigy. The ensuing midnight, they heard great cries and clamour from the Cave, resounding like the noise of Battle, and the ground shaking with a tremendous roar ; the whole edifice of the old Tower fell to the ground, by which they were greatly affrighted, the Vision which they had beheld appearing to them as a dream."

Scott's poem on the Field of Waterloo was written to assist the Waterloo subscription.

H. M.

The Pike County Ballads.

JIM BLUDSO,

OF THE "PRAIRIE BELLE."

WALL, no! I can't tell whar he lives,
  Becase he don't live, you see;
Leastways, he's got out of the habit
  Of livin' like you and me.
Whar have you been for the last three year
  That you haven't heard folks tell
How Jimmy Bludso passed in his checks
  The night of the *Prairie Belle?*

He weren't no saint,—them engineers
  Is all pretty much alike,—
One wife in Natchez-under-the-Hill,
  And another one here, in Pike;
A keerless man in his talk was Jim,
  And an awkward hand in a row,
But he never flunked, and he never lied,—
  I reckon he never knowed how.

And this was all the religion he had,—
  To treat his engine well;
Never be passed on the river;
  To mind the pilot's bell;
And if ever the *Prairie Belle* took fire,—
  A thousand times he swore,
He'd hold her nozzle agin the bank
  Till the last soul got ashore.

13

All boats has their day on the Mississip,
  And her day come at last,—
The *Movastar* was a better boat,
  But the *Belle* she *wouldn't* be passed.
And so she come tearin' along that night—
  The oldest craft on the line—
With a nigger squat on her safety-valve,
  And her furnace crammed, rosin and pine.

The fire bust out as she clared the bar,
  And burnt a hole in the night,
And quick as a flash she turned, and made
  For that willer-bank on the right.
There was runnin' and cursin', but Jim yelled out,
  Over all the infernal roar,
" I'll hold her nozzle agin the bank
  Till the last galoot's ashore."

Through the hot, black breath of the burnin' boat
  Jim Bludso's voice was heard,
And they all had trust in his cussedness,
  And knowed he would keep his word.
And, sure's you're born, they all got off
  Afore the smokestacks fell,—
And Bludso's ghost went up alone
  In the smoke of the *Prairie Belle*.

He weren't no saint,—but at jedgment
  I'd run my chance with Jim,
'Longside of some pious gentlemen
  That wouldn't shook hands with him.
He seen his duty, a dead-sure thing,—
  And went for it thar and then ;
And Christ ain't a-going to be too hard
  On a man that died for men.

LITTLE BREECHES.

I DON'T go much on religion,
  I never ain't had no show;
But I've got a middlin' tight grip, sir,
  On the handful o' things I know.
I don't pan out on the prophets
  And free-will, and that sort of thing,—
But I b'lieve in God and the angels,
  Ever sence one night last spring.

I come into town with some turnips,
  And my little Gabe come along,—
No four-year-old in the county
  Could beat him for pretty and strong,
Peart and chipper and sassy,
  Always ready to swear and fight,—
And I'd larnt him to chaw terbacker
  Jest to keep his milk-teeth white.

The snow come down like a blanket
  As I passed by Taggart's store;
I went in for a jug of molasses
  And left the team at the door.
They scared at something and started,—
  I heard one little squall,
And hell-to-split over the prairie
  Went team, Little Breeches and all.

Hell-to-split over the prairie!
  I was almost froze with skeer;
But we rousted up some torches,
  And searched for 'em far and near.
At last we struck hosses and wagon,
  Snowed under a soft white mound,
Upsot, dead beat,—but of little Gabe
  No hide nor hair was found.

And here all hope soured on me,
    Of my fellow-critters' aid,—
I jest flopped down on my marrow-bones,
    Crotch-deep in the snow, and prayed.

    .   .   .   .   .   .

By this, the torches was played out,
    And me and Isrul Parr
Went off for some wood to a sheepfold
    That he said was somewhar thar.

We found it at last, and a little shed
    Where they shut up the lambs at night.
We looked in and seen them huddled thar,
    So warm and sleepy and white;
And thar sot Little Breeches and chirped,
    As peart as. ever you see,
" I want a chaw of terbacker,
    And that's what's the matter of me."

How did he git thar? Angels.
    He could never have walked in that storm;
They jest scooped down and toted him
    To whar it was safe and warm.
And I think that saving a little child,
    And fotching him to his own,
Is a derned sight better business
    Than loafing around The Throne.

BANTY TIM.

REMARKS OF SERGEANT TILMON JOY TO THE
WHITE MAN'S COMMITTEE OF SPUNKY POINT,
ILLINOIS.

I RECKON I git your drift, gents,—
    You 'low the boy sha'n't stay;
This is a white man's country;
    You're Dimocrats, you say;
And whereas, and seein', and wherefore,
    The times bein' all out o' j'int,
The nigger has got to mosey
    From the limits o' Spunky P'int!

Le's reason the thing a minute:
    I'm an old-fashioned Dimocrat too,
Though I laid my politics out o' the way
    For to keep till the war was through.
But I come back here, allowin'
    To vote as I used to do,
Though it gravels me like the devil to train
    Along o' sich fools as you.

Now dog my cats ef I kin see,
    In all the light of the day,
What you've got to do with the question
    Ef Tim shill go or stay.
And furder than that I give notice,
    Ef one of you tetches the boy,
He kin check his trunks to a warmer clime
    Than he'll find in Illanoy.

Why, blame your hearts, jest hear me!
    You know that ungodly day
When our left struck Vicksburg Heights, how
        ripped
    And torn and tattered we lay.

When the rest retreated I stayed behind,
  Fur reasons sufficient to me,—
With a rib caved in, and a leg on a strike,
  I sprawled on that cursed glacee.

Lord! how the hot sun went for us,
  And br'iled and blistered and burned!
How the Rebel bullets whizzed round us
  When a cuss in his death-grip turned!
Till along toward dusk I seen a thing
  I couldn't believe for a spell:
That nigger—that Tim—was a crawlin' to me
  Through that fire-proof, gilt-edged hell!

The Rebels seen him as quick as me,
  And the bullets buzzed like bees;
But he jumped for me, and shouldered me,
  Though a shot brought him once to his knees;
But he staggered up, and packed me off,
  With a dozen stumbles and falls,
Till safe in our lines he drapped us both,
  His black hide riddled with balls.

So, my gentle gazelles, thar's my answer,
  And here stays Banty Tim:
He trumped Death's ace for me that day,
  And I'm not goin' back on him!
You may rezoloot till the cows come home,
  But ef one of you tetches the boy,
He'll wrastle his hash to-night in hell,
  Or my name's not Tilmon Joy!

THE MYSTERY OF GILGAL.

The darkest, strangest mystery
I ever read, or heern, or see,
Is 'long of a drink at Taggart's Hall,—
Tom Taggart's of Gilgal.

I've heern the tale a thousand ways,
But never could git through the maze
That hangs around that queer day's doin's ;
But I'll tell the yarn to youans.

Tom Taggart stood behind his bar,
The time was fall, the skies was fa'r,
The neighbours round the counter drawed,
And ca'mly drinked and jawed.

At last come Colonel Blood of Pike,
And old Jedge Phinn, permiscus-like,
And each, as he meandered in,
Remarked, "A whisky-skin."

Tom mixed the beverage full and fa'r,
And slammed it, smoking, on the bar.
Some says three fingers, some says two,—
I'll leave the choice to you.

Phinn to the drink put forth his hand ;
Blood drawed his knife, with accent bland,
"I ax yer parding, Mister Phinn—
Jest drap that whisky-skin."

No man high-toneder could be found
Than old Jedge Phinn the country round.
Says he, "Young man, the tribe of Phinns
Knows their own whisky-skins !"

He went for his 'leven-inch bowie-knife :—
" I tries to foller a Christian life ;
But I'll drap a slice of liver or two,
   My bloomin' shrub, with you."

They carved in a way that all admired,
Tell Blood drawed iron at last, and fired.
It took Seth Bludso 'twixt the eyes,
   Which caused him great surprise.

Then coats went off, and all went in ;
Shots and bad language swelled the din ;
The short, sharp bark of Derringers,
   Like bull-pups, cheered the furse.

They piled the stiffs outside the door ;
They made, I reckon, a cord or more.
Girls went that winter, as a rule,
   Alone to spellin'-school.

I've searched in vain, from Dan to Beer-
Sheba, to make this mystery clear ;
But I end with *hit* as I did begin,—
   " WHO GOT THE WHISKY-SKIN ? "

GOLYER.

EF the way a man lights out of this world
   Helps fix his heft for the other sp'ere,
I reckon my old friend Golyer's Ben
Will lay over lots of likelier men
   For one thing he done down here.

You didn't know Ben?   He driv a stage
   On the line they called the Old Sou'-west ;
He wa'n't the best man that ever you seen,
And he wa'n't so ungodly pizen mean,—
   No better nor worse than the rest.

He was hard on women and rough on his friends;
  And he didn't have many, I'll let you know;
He hated a dog and disgusted a cat,
But he'd run off his legs for a motherless brat,
  And I guess there's many jess so.

I've seed my sheer of the run of things,
  I've hoofed it a many and many a miled,
But I never seed nothing that could or can
Jest git all the good from the heart of a man
  Like the hands of a little child.

Weil! this young one I started to tell you about,—
  His folks was all dead, I was fetchin' him
    through,—
He was just at the age that's loudest for boys,
And he blowed such a horn with his sarchin' small
    voice,
  We called him "the Little Boy Blue."

He ketched a sight of Ben on the box,
  And you bet he bawled and kicked and howled,
For to git 'long of Ben, and ride thar too;
I tried to tell him it wouldn't do,
  When suddingly Golyer growled,

"What's the use of making the young one cry?
  Say, what's the use of being a fool?
Sling the little one up here whar he can see,
He won't git the snuffles a-ridin' with me,—
  The night ain't any too cool."

The child hushed cryin' the minute he spoke;
  "Come up here, Major! don't let him slip."
And jest as nice as a woman could do,
He wropped his blanket around them two,
  And was off in the crack of a whip.

We rattled along an hour or so,
  Till we heerd a yell on the still night air.
Did you ever hear an Apache yell?
Well, ye needn't want to, *this* side of hell;
  There's nothing more devilish there.

Caught in the shower of lead and flint,
    We felt the old stage stagger and plunge ;
Then we heerd the voice and the whip of Ben,
As he gethered his critters up again,
    And tore away with a lunge.

The passengers laughed. " Old Ben's all right,
    He's druv five year and never was struck."
" Now if *I*'d been thar, as sure as you live,
They'd 'a' plugged me with holes as thick as a
        sieve ;
    It's the reg'lar Golyer luck."

Over hill and holler and ford and creek,
    Jest like the hosses had wings, we tore ;
We got to Looney's, and Ben come in
And laid down the baby and axed for his gin,
    And dropped in a heap on the floor.

Said he, " When they fired, I kivered the kid,—
    Although I ain't pretty, I'm middlin' broad ;
And look ! he ain't fazed by arrow nor ball,—
Thank God ! my own carcase stopped them all."
Then we seen his eye glaze, and his lower jaw fall,—
    And he carried his thanks to God.

—◦◦◦—

THE PLEDGE AT SPUNKY POINT.

A TALE OF EARNEST EFFORT AND HUMAN PERFIDY.

It's all very well for preachin',
    But preachin' and practice don't gee :
I've give the thing a fair trial,
    And you can't ring it in on me.
So toddle along with your pledge, Squire,
    Ef that's what you want me to sign ;
Betwixt me and you, I've been thar,
    And I'll not take any in mine.

A year ago last Fo'th July
  A lot of the boys was here,
We all got corned and signed the pledge
  For to drink no more that year.
There was Tilmon Joy and Sheriff McPhail
  And me and Abner Fry,
And Shelby's boy Leviticus,
  And the Golyers, Luke and Cy.

And we anteed up a hundred
  In the hands of Deacon Kedge
For to be divided the follerin' Fo'th
  'Mongst the boys that kep' the pledge.
And we knowed each other so well, Squire,
  You may take my scalp for a fool,
Ef every man when he signed his name
  Didn't feel cock-sure of the pool.

Fur a while it all went lovely ;
  We put up a job next day
Fur to make Joy b'lieve his wife was dead,
  And he went home middlin' gay ;
Then Abner Fry he killed a man
  And afore he was hung McPhail
Jest bilked the widder outen her sheer
  By getting him slewed in jail.

But Chris'mas scooped the Sheriff,
  The egg-nogs gethered him in ;
And Shelby's boy Leviticus
  Was, New Year's, tight as sin ;
And along in March the Golyers
  Got so drunk that a fresh-biled owl
Would 'a' looked 'longside o' them two young
      men,
  Like a sober temperance fowl.

Four months alone I walked the chalk,
  I thought my heart would break ;
And all them boys a-slappin' my back
  And axin', "What'll you take?"

I never slep' without dreamin' dreams
    Of Burbin, Peach, or Rye,
But I chawed at my niggerhead and swore
    I'd rake that pool or die.

At last—the Fo'th—I humped myself
    Through chores and breakfast soon,
Then scooted down to Taggart's store—
    For the pledge was off at noon ;
And all the boys was gethered thar,
    And each man hilt his glass—
Watchin' me and the clock quite solemn-like
    Fur to see the last minute pass.

The clock struck twelve !   I raised the jug
    And took one lovin' pull—
I was holler clar from skull to boots.
    It seemed I couldn't git full.
But I was roused by a fiendish laugh
    That might have raised the dead—
Them ornary sneaks had sot the clock
    A half an hour ahead !

"All right !" I squawked.   "You've got me,
    Jest order your drinks agin,
And we'll paddle up to the Deacon's
    And scoop the ante in."
But when we got to Kedge's,
    What a sight was that we saw !
The Deacon and Parson Skeeters
    In the tail of a game of Draw.

They had shook 'em the heft of the mornin',
    The Parson's luck was fa'r,
And he raked, the minute we got thar,
    The last of our pool on a pa'r.
So toddie along with your pledge, Squire,
    I 'low it's all very fine,
But ez fur myself, I thank ye,
    I'll not take any in mine.

Wanderlieder.

—⚬⚬⚬—

SUNRISE IN THE PLACE DE LA CONCORDE.

(PARIS, AUGUST 1865.)

I STAND at the break of day
In the Champs Elysées.
The tremulous shafts of dawning,
As they shoot o'er the Tuileries early,
Strike Luxor's cold grey spire,
And wild in the light of the morning
With their marble manes on fire,
Ramp the white Horses of Marly.

But the Place of Concord lies
Dead hushed 'neath the ashy skies.
And the Cities sit in council
With sleep in their wide stone eyes.
I see the mystic plain
Where the army of spectres slain
In the Emperor's life-long war
March on with unsounding tread
To trumpets whose voice is dead.
Their spectral chief still leads them,—
The ghostly flash of his sword
Like a comet through mist shines far,—
And the noiseless host is poured,
For the gendarme never heeds them,
Up the long dim road where thundered
The army of Italy onward
Through the great pale Arch of the Star !

The spectre army fades
Far up the glimmering hill,
But, vaguely lingering still,
A group of shuddering shades
Infects the pallid air,
Growing dimmer as day invades
The hush of the dusky square.
There is one that seems a King,
As if the ghost of a Crown
Still shadowed his jail-bleached hair;
I can hear the guillotine ring,
As its regicide note rang there,
When he laid his tired life down
And grew brave in his last despair.
And a woman frail and fair
Who weeps at leaving a world
Of love and revel and sin
In the vast Unknown to be hurled;
(For life was wicked and sweet
With kings at her small white feet!)
And one, every inch a Queen,
In life and in death a Queen,
Whose blood baptized the place,
In the days of madness and fear,—
Her shade has never a peer
In majesty and grace.

Murdered and murderers swarm;
Slayers that slew and were slain,
Till the drenched place smoked with the
    rain
That poured in a torrent warm,—
Till red as the Riders of Edom
Were splashed the white garments of
    Freedom
With the wash of the horrible storm!

And Liberty's hands were not clean
In the day of her pride unchained,
Her royal hands were stained
With the life of a King and Queen;

And darker than that with the blood
Of the nameless brave and good
Whose blood in witness clings
More damning than Queens' and Kings'.

Has she not paid it dearly?
Chained, watching her chosen nation
Grinding late and early
In the mills of usurpation?
Have not her holy tears,
Flowing through shameful years,
Washed the stains from her tortured hands?
We thought so when God's fresh breeze,
Blowing over the sleeping lands,
In 'Forty-Eight waked the world,
And the Burgher-King was hurled
From that palace behind the trees.

As Freedom with eyes aglow
Smiled glad through her childbirth pain,
How was the mother to know
That her woe and travail were vain?
A smirking servant smiled
When she gave him her child to keep ;
Did she know he would strangle the child
As it lay in his arms asleep?

Liberty's cruellest shame !
She is stunned and speechless yet,
In her grief and bloody sweat
Shall we make her trust her blame?
The treasure of 'Forty-Eight
A lurking jail-bird stole,
She can but watch and wait
As the swift sure seasons roll.

And when in God's good hour
Comes the time of the brave and true,
Freedom again shall rise
With a blaze in her awful eyes
That shall wither this robber-power
As the sun now dries the dew.

This Place shall roar with the voice
Of the glad triumphant people,
And the heavens be gay with the chimes
Ringing with jubilant noise
From every clamorous steeple
The coming of better times.
And the dawn of Freedom waking
Shall fling its splendours far
Like the day which now is breaking
On the great pale Arch of the Star,
And back o'er the town shall fly,
While the joy-bells wild are ringing,
To crown the Glory springing
From the Column of July !

—◦⊱◦—

THE SPHINX OF THE TUILERIES.

Out of the Latin Quarter
  I came to the lofty door
Where the two marble Sphinxes guard
  The Pavillon de Flore.
Two Cockneys stood by the gate, and one
  Observed, as they turned to go,
" No wonder He likes that sort of thing,—
  He's a Sphinx himself, you know."

I thought as I walked where the garden glowed
  In the sunset's level fire,
Of the Charlatan whom the Frenchmen loathe
  And the Cockneys all admire.
They call him a Sphinx,—it pleases him,—
  And if we narrowly read,
We will find some truth in the flunkey's praise,—
  The man is a Sphinx indeed.

For the Sphinx with breast of woman
  And face so debonair
Had the sleek false paws of a lion,
  That could furtively seize and tear.

So far to the shoulders,—but if you took
    The Beast in reverse you would find
The ignoble form of a craven cur
    Was all that lay behind.

She lived by giving to simple folk
    A silly riddle to read,
And when they failed she drank their blood
    In cruel and ravenous greed.
But at last came one who knew her word,
    And she perished in pain and shame,—
This bastard Sphinx leads the same base
    life
    And his end will be the same.

For an Œdipus-People is coming fast
    With swelled feet limping on,
If they shout his true name once aloud .
    His false foul power is gone.
Afraid to fight and afraid to fly,
    He cowers in an abject shiver ;
The people will come to their own at
    last,—
    God is not mocked for ever.

THE SURRENDER OF SPAIN.

I.

LAND of unconquered Pelayo ! land of the Cid
    Campeador !
Sea-girdled mother of men ! Spain, name of glory
    and power ;
Cradle of world-grasping Emperors, grave of the
    reckless invader,
How art thou fallen, my Spain ! how art thou sunk
    at this hour !

II.

Once thy magnanimous sons trod, victors, the
 portals of Asia,
Once the Pacific waves rushed, joyful thy banners
 to see ;
For it was Trajan that carried the battle-flushed
 eagles to Dacia,
Cortés that planted thy flag fast by the uttermost
 sea.

III.

Hast thou forgotten those days illumined with glory
 and honour,
When the far isles of the sea thrilled to the tread
 of Castile ?
When every land under Heaven was flecked by the
 shade of thy banner,--
When every beam of the sun flashed on thy conquering steel ?

IV.

Then through red fields of slaughter, through death
 and defeat and disaster,
Still flared thy banner aloft, tattered, but free from
 a stain,--
Now to the upstart Savoyard thou bendest to beg
 for a master !
How the red flush of her shame mars the proud
 beauty of Spain !

V.

Has the red blood run cold that boiled by the
 Xenil and Darro ?
Are the high deeds of the sires sung to the children
 no more ?
On the dun hills of the North hast thou heard of
 no plough-boy Pizarro ?
Roams no young swine-herd Cortés hid by the
 Tagus' wild shore ?

VI.

Once again does Hispania bend low to the yoke of
   the stranger!
Once again will she rise, flinging her gyves in the
   sea!
Princeling of Piedmont! unwitting thou weddest
   with doubt and with danger,
King over men who have learned all that it costs
   to be free.

THE PRAYER OF THE ROMANS.

Not done, but near its ending,
   Is the work that our eyes desired ;
Not yet fulfilled, but near the goal,
   Is the hope that our worn hearts fired.
And on the Alban Mountains,
   Where the blushes of dawn increase,
We see the flash of the beautiful feet
   Of Freedom and of Peace!

How long were our fond dreams baffled !—
   Novara's sad mischance,
The Kaiser's sword and fetter-lock;
   And the traitor stab of France ;
Till at last came glorious Venice,
   In storm and tempest home ;
And now God maddens the greedy kings,
   And gives to her people Rome.

Lame Lion of Caprera !
   Red-shirts of the lost campaigns !
Not idly shed was the costly blood
   You poured from generous veins.
For the shame of Aspromonte,
   And the stain of Mentana's sod,
But forged the curse of kings that sprang
   From your breaking hearts to God !

We lift our souls to Thee, O Lord
  Of Liberty and of Light !
Let not earth's kings pollute the work
  That was done in their despite ;
Let not Thy light be darkened
  In the shade of a sordid crown,
Nor pampered swine devour the fruit
  Thou shook'st with an earthquake down !

Let the People come to their birthright,
  And crosier and crown pass away
Like phantasms that flit o'er the marshes
  At the glance of the clean, white day.
And then from the lava of Ætna
  To the ice of the Alps let there be
One freedom, one faith without fetters,
  One republic in Italy free !

THE CURSE OF HUNGARY.

KING SALOMAN looked from his donjon bars,
  Where the Danube clamours through sedge and
    sand,
  And he cursed with a curse his revolting land,—
With a king's deep curse of treason and wars.

He said : " May this false land know no truth !
  May the good hearts die and the bad ones
    flourish,
  And a greed of glory but live to nourish
Envy and hate in its restless youth.

" In the barren soil may the ploughshare rust,
  While the sword grows bright with its fatal labour,
  And blackens between each man and neighbour
The perilous cloud of a vague distrust !

" Be the noble idle, the peasant in thrall,
And each to the other as unknown things,
That with links of hatred and pride the kings
May forge firm fetters through each for all !

" May a king wrong them as they wronged their
king !
May he wring their hearts as they wrung mine,
Till they pour their blood for his revels like wine,
And to women and monks their birthright fling ! "

The mad king died ; but the rushing river
Still brawls by the spot where his donjon stands,
And its swift waves sigh to the conscious sands
That the curse of King Saloman works for ever.

For flowing by Pressbourg they heard the cheers
Ring out from the leal and cheated hearts
That were caught and chained by Theresa's arts,—
A man's cool head and a girl's hot tears !

And a star, scarce risen, they saw decline,
Where Orsova's hills looked coldly down,
As Kossuth buried the Iron Crown
And fled in the dark to the Turkish line.

And latest they saw in the summer glare
The Magyar nobles in pomp arrayed,
To shout as they saw, with his unfleshed blade,
A Hapsburg beating the harmless air.

But ever the same sad play they saw,
The same weak worship of sword and crown,
The noble crushing the humble down,
And moulding Wrong to a monstrous Law.

The donjon stands by the turbid river,
But Time is crumbling its battered towers ;
And the slow light withers a despot's powers,
And a mad king's curse is not for ever !

B 2

THE MONKS OF BASLE.

I TORE this weed from the rank, dark soil
  Where it grew in the monkish time,
I trimmed it close and set it again
  In a border of modern rhyme.

1.

Long years ago, when the Devil was loose
  And faith was sorely tried,
Three monks of Basle went out to walk
  In the quiet eventide.

A breeze as pure as the breath of Heaven
  Blew fresh through the cloister-shades,
A sky as glad as the smile of Heaven
  Blushed rose o'er the minster-glades.

But scorning the lures of summer and sense,
  The monks passed on in their walk ;
Their eyes were abased, their senses slept,
  Their souls were in their talk.

In the tough grim talk of the monkish days
  They hammered and slashed about,—
Dry husks of logic,—old scraps of creed,—
  And the cold gray dreams of doubt,—

And whether Just or Justified
  Was the Church's mystic Head,—
And whether the Bread was changed to God,
  Or God became the Bread.

But of human hearts outside their walls
  They never paused to dream,
And they never thought of the love of God
  That smiled in the twilight gleam.

II.

As these three monks went bickering on
  By the foot of a spreading tree,
Out from its heart of verdurous gloom
  A song burst wild and free,—

A wordless carol of life and love,
  Of nature free and wild ;
And the three monks paused in the evening shade,
  Looked up at each other and smiled.

And tender and gay the bird sang on,
  And cooed and whistled and trilled,
And the wasteful wealth of life and love
  From his happy heart was spilled.

The song had power on the grim old monks
  In the light of the rosy skies ;
And as they listened the years rolled back,
  And tears came into their eyes.

The years rolled back and they were young,
  With the hearts and hopes of men,
They plucked the daisies and kissed the girls
  Of dear dead summers again.

III.

But the eldest monk soon broke the spell ;
  " 'Tis sin and shame," quoth he,
" To be turned from talk of holy things
  By a bird's cry from a tree.

" Perchance the Enemy of Souls
  Hath come to tempt us so.
Let us try by the power of the Awful Word
  If it be he, or no ! "

To Heaven the three monks raised their hands ;
  " We charge thee, speak ! " they said,
" By His dread Name who shall one day come
  To judge the quick and the dead,—

"Who art thou? Speak!" The bird laughed
    loud.
  "I am the Devil," he said.
The monks on their faces fell, the bird
    Away through the twilight sped.

A horror fell on those holy men
    (The faithful legends say),
And one by one from the face of the earth
    They pined and vanished away.

IV.

So goes the tale of the monkish books,
    The moral who runs may read,—
He has no ears for Nature's voice
    Whose soul is the slave of creed.

Not all in vain with beauty and love
    Has God the world adorned;
And he who Nature scorns and mocks,
    By Nature is mocked and scorned,

—⁂—

THE ENCHANTED SHIRT.

Fytte the First : *wherein it shall be shown how the
Truth is too mighty a Drug for such as be of
feeble temper.*

THE King was sick. His cheek was red
    And his eye was clear and bright;
He ate and drank with a kingly zest,
    And peacefully snored at night.

But he said he was sick, and a king should know,
    And doctors came by the score.
They did not cure him. He cut off their heads
    And sent to the schools for more.

At last two famous doctors came,
  And one was as poor as a rat,—
He had passed his life in studious toil,
  And never found time to grow fat.

The other had never looked in a book ;
  His patients gave him no trouble—
If they recovered they paid him well,
  If they died their heirs paid double.

Together they looked at the royal tongue,
  As the King on his couch reclined ;
In succession they thumped his august chest,
  But no trace of disease could find.

The old sage said, "You're as sound as a nut."
  "Hang him up !" roared the King in a gale,—
In a ten-knot gale of royal rage ;
  The other leech grew a shade pale ;

But he pensively rubbed his sagacious nose,
  And thus his prescription ran,—
*The King will be well, if he sleeps one night
In the Shirt of a Happy Man.*

Fytte the Second : *tells of the search for the Shirt,
  and how it was nigh found, but was not, for
  reasons which are said or sung.*

Wide o'er the realm the couriers rode,
  And fast their horses ran,
And many they saw, and to many they spoke,
  But they found no Happy Man.

They found poor men who would fain be rich
  And rich who thought they were poor ;
And men who twisted their waists in stays,
  And women that shorthose wore.

They saw two men by the roadside sit,
　And both bemoaned their lot ;
For one had buried his wife, he said,
　And the other one had not.

At last they came to a village gate,
　A beggar lay whistling there ;
He whistled and sang and laughed and rolled
　On the grass in the soft June air.

The weary couriers paused and looked
　At the scamp so blithe and gay ;
And one of them said, " Heaven save you, friend !
　You seem to be happy to-day."

" O yes, fair sirs !" the rascal laughed,
　And his voice rang free and glad,
" An idle man has so much to do
　That he never has time to be sad."

" This is our man," the courier said ;
　" Our luck has led us aright.
" I will give you a hundred ducats, friend,
　For the loan of your shirt to-night."

The merry blackguard lay back on the grass,
　And laughed till his face was black ;
" I would do it, God wot," and he roared with the
　　fun,
　" But I haven't a shirt to my back."

Fytte the Third : *shewing how His Majesty the
　King came at last to sleep in a Happy Man
　his Shirt.*

Each day to the King the reports came in
　Of his unsuccessful spies,
And the sad panorama of human woes
　Passed daily under his eyes.

And he grew ashamed of his useless life,
  And his maladies hatched in gloom ;
He opened his windows and let the air
  Of the free heaven into his room.

And out he went in the world and toiled
  In his own appointed way ;
And the people blessed him, the land was glad,
  And the King was well and gay.

A WOMAN'S LOVE.

A SENTINEL angel sitting high in glory
Heard this shrill wail ring out from Purgatory :
" Have mercy, mighty angel, hear my story !

" I loved,—and, blind with passionate love, I fell.
Love brought me down to death, and death to Hell.
For God is just, and death for sin is well.

" I do not rage against His high decree,
Nor for myself do ask that grace shall be ;
But for my love on earth who mourns for me.

" Great Spirit ! let me see my love again
And comfort him one hour, and I were fain
To pay a thousand years of fire and pain."

Then said the pitying angel, " Nay, repent
That wild vow ! Look, the dial-finger's bent
Down to the last hour of thy punishment !"

But still she wailed, " I pray thee, let me go !
I cannot rise to peace and leave him so.
Oh, let me soothe him in his bitter woe !"

The brazen gates ground sullenly ajar,
And upward, joyous, like a rising star,
She rose and vanished in the ether far.

But soon adown the dying sunset sailing,
And like a wounded bird her pinions trailing,
She fluttered back, with broken-hearted wailing.

She sobbed, "I found him by the summer sea
Reclined, his head upon a maiden's knee,—
She curled his hair and kissed him. Woe is me!

She wept, "Now let my punishment begin!
I have been fond and foolish. Let me in
To expiate my sorrow and my sin."

The angel answered, "Nay, sad soul, go higher!
To be deceived in your true heart's desire
Was bitterer than a thousand years of fire!"

ON PITZ LANGUARD.

I STOOD on the top of Pitz Languard,
  And heard three voices whispering low,
Where the Alpine birds in their circling ward
  Made swift dark shadows upon the snow.

First Voice.

I loved a girl with truth and pain,
  She loved me not. When she said good-bye
She gave me a kiss to sting and stain
  My broken life to a rosy dye.

Second Voice.

I loved a woman with love well tried,—
  And I swear I believe she loves me still.
But it was not I who stood by her side
  When she answered the priest and said " I will."

Third Voice.

I loved two girls, one fond, one shy,
  And I never divined which one loved me.
One married, and now, though I can't tell why,
  Of the four in the story I count but three.

The three weird voices whispered low
  Where the eagles swept in their circling ward ;
But only one shadow scarred the snow
  As I clambered down from Pitz Languard.

BOUDOIR PROPHECIES.

ONE day in the Tuileries,
When a south-west Spanish breeze
    Brought scandalous news of the Queen,
The fair, proud Empress said,
"My good friend loses her head ;
  If matters go on this way,
  I shall see her shopping, some day,
    In the Boulevard des Capucines."

The saying swiftly went
To the Place of the Orient,
    And the stout Queen sneered, "Ah, well!
    You are proud and prude, ma belle !
But I think I will hazard a guess
I shall see you one day playing chess
    With the Curé of Carabanchel."

Both ladies, though not over wise,
Were lucky in prophecies.
  For the Boulevard shopmen well
  Know the form of stout Isabel
    As she buys her modes de Paris ;
And after Sedan in despair
The Empress prude and fair
Went to visit Madame sa Mère
  In her villa at Carabanchel—
    But the Queen was not there to see.

A TRIUMPH OF ORDER

A SQUAD of regular infantry,
   In the Commune's closing days,
Had captured a crowd of rebels
   By the wall of Père-la-Chaise.

There were desperate men, wild women,
   And dark-eyed Amazon girls,
And one little boy, with a peach-down cheek
   And yellow clustering curls.

The captain seized the little waif,
   And said, "What dost thou here?"
"Sapristi, Citizen captain!
   I'm a Communist, my dear!"

"Very well! Then you die with the others!"
   —"Very well! That's my affair;
But first let me take to my mother,
   Who lives by the wine-shop there,

"My father's watch. You see it;
   A gay old thing, is it not?
It would please the old lady to have it;
   Then I'll come back here, and be shot."

"That is the last we shall see of him,"
   The grizzled captain grinned,
As the little man skimmed down the hill
   Like a swallow down the wind.

For the joy of killing had lost its zest
   In the glut of those awful days,
And Death writhed, gorged like a greedy snake,
   From the Arch to Père-la-Chaise.

But before the last platoon had fired
  The child's shrill voice was heard ;
" Houp-là ! the old girl made such a row
  I feared I should break my word."

Against the bullet-pitted wall
  He took his place with the rest,
A button was lost from his ragged blouse,
  Which showed his soft white breast.

" Now blaze away, my children !
  With your little one-two-three ! "
The Chassepots tore the stout young heart,
  And saved Society.

—◦◦◦—

ERNST OF EDELSHEIM.

I'LL tell the story, kissing
  This white hand for my pains :
No sweeter heart, nor falser,
  E'er filled such fine, blue veins.

I'll sing a song of true love,
  My Lilith, dear ! to you ;
Contraria contrariis—
  The rule is old and true.

The happiest of all lovers
  Was Ernst of Edelsheim ;
And why he was the happiest,
  I'll tell you in my rhyme.

One summer night he wandered
  Within a lonely glade,
And, couched in moss and moonlight,
  He found a sleeping maid.

The stars of midnight sifted
  Above her sands of gold;
She seemed a slumbering statue,
  So fair and white and cold.

Fair and white and cold she lay
  Beneath the starry skies;
Rosy was her waking
  Beneath the Ritter's eyes.

He won her drowsy fancy,
  He bore her to his towers,
And swift with love and laughter
  Flew morning's purpled hours.

But when the thickening sunbeams
  Had drunk the gleaming dew,
A misty cloud of sorrow
  Swept o'er her eyes' deep blue.

She hung upon the Ritter's neck,
  She wept with love and pain,
She showered her sweet, warm kisses
  Like fragrant summer rain.

"I am no Christian soul," she sobbed,
  As in his arms she lay;
"I'm half the day a woman,
  A serpent half the day.

"And when from yonder bell-tower
  Rings out the noonday chime,
Farewell! farewell for ever,
  Sir Ernst of Edelsheim!"

"Ah! not farewell for ever!"
  The Ritter wildly cried;
"I will be saved or lost with thee,
  My lovely Wili-Bride!"

Loud from the lordly bell-tower
  Rang out the noon of day,
And from the bower of roses
  A serpent slid away.

But when the mid-watch moonlight
  Was shimmering through the grove,
He clasped his bride thrice dowered
  With beauty and with love.

The happiest of all lovers
  Was Ernst of Edelsheim—
His true love was a serpent
  Only half the time !

MY CASTLE IN SPAIN.

THERE was never a castle seen
  So fair as mine in Spain :
It stands embowered in green,
  Crowning the gentle slope
Of a hill by the Xenil's shore
And at eve its shade flaunts o'er
  The storied Vega plain,
And its towers are hid in the mists of Hope ;
  And I toil through years of pain
  Its glimmering gates to gain.

In visions wild and sweet
Sometimes its courts I greet :
  Sometimes in joy its shining halls
I tread with favoured feet ;
But never my eyes in the light of day
  Were blest with its ivied walls,
Where the marble white and the granite gray
Turn gold alike when the sunbeams play,
  When the soft day dimly falls.

I know in its dusky rooms
  Are treasures rich and rare;
The spoil of Eastern looms,
  And whatever of bright and fair
Painters divine have caught and won
  From the vault of Italy's air:
White gods in Phidian stone
  People the haunted glooms;
And the song of immortal singers
Like a fragrant memory lingers,
  I know, in the echoing rooms.

But nothing of these, my soul!
  Nor castle, nor treasures, nor skies,
Nor the waves of the river that roll
  With a cadence faint and sweet
  In peace by its marble feet—
Nothing of these is the goal
  For which my whole heart sighs.
'Tis the pearl gives worth to the shell—
  The pearl I would die to gain;
For there does my lady dwell,
My love that I love so well—
  The Queen whose gracious reign
  Makes glad my castle in Spain.

Her face so pure and fair
  Sheds light in the shady places,
And the spell of her girlish graces
  Holds charmed the happy air.
A breath of purity
  For ever before her flies,
And ill things cease to be
  In the glance of her honest eyes.
Around her pathway flutter,
  Where her dear feet wander free
  In youth's pure majesty,
  The wings of the vague desires;
But the thought that love would utter
  In reverence expires.

Not yet! not yet shall I see
  That face which shines like a star
  O'er my storm-swept life afar,
Transfigured with love for me.
Toiling, forgetting, and learning
With labour and vigils and prayers,
  Pure heart and resolute will,
  At last I shall climb the hill
And breathe the enchanted airs
Where the light of my life is burning
  Most lovely and fair and free,
Where alone in her youth and beauty
And bound by her fate's sweet duty,
  Unconscious she waits for me.

SISTER SAINT LUKE.

SHE lived shut in by flowers and trees
And shade of gentle bigotries.
On this side lay the trackless sea,
On that the great world's mystery;
But all unseen and all unguessed
They could not break upon her rest.
The world's far splendours gleamed and flashed,
Afar the wild seas foamed and dashed;
But in her small, dull Paradise,
Safe housed from rapture or surprise,
Nor day nor night had power to fright
The peace of God that filled her eyes.

New and Old.

—◦≫◦—

MILES KEOGH'S HORSE.

On the bluff of the Little Big-Horn,
　At the close of a woeful day,
Custer and his Three Hundred
　In death and silence lay.

Three Hundred to Three Thousand!
　They had bravely fought and bled;
For such is the will of Congress
　When the White man meets the Red.

The White men are ten millions,
　The thriftiest under the sun;
The Reds are fifty thousand,
　And warriors every one.

So Custer and all his fighting-men
　Lay under the evening skies,
Staring up at the tranquil heaven
　With wide, accusing eyes.

And of all that stood at noonday
　In that fiery scorpion ring,
Miles Keogh's horse at evening
　Was the only living thing.

Alone from that field of slaughter,
　Where lay the three hundred slain,
The horse Comanche wandered,
　With Keogh's blood on his mane.

And Sturgis issued this order,
　　Which future times shall read,
While the love and honour of comrades
　　Are the soul of the soldier's creed.

He said—

　　　Let the horse Comanche
　　Henceforth till he shall die,
Be kindly cherished and cared for
　　By the Seventh Cavalry.

He shall do no labour ; he never shall know
　　The touch of spur or rein ;
Nor shall his back be ever crossed
　　By living rider again.

And at regimental formation
　　Of the Seventh Cavalry,
Comanche draped in mourning and led
　　By a trooper of Company I,

Shall parade with the Regiment !
　　　　　　　　　Thus it was
　　Commanded and thus done,
By order of General Sturgis, signed
　　By Adjutant Garlington.

Even as the sword of Custer,
　　In his disastrous fall,
Flashed out a blaze that charmed the world
　　And glorified his pall,

This order, issued amid the gloom
　　That shrouds our army's name,
When all foul beasts are free to rend
　　And tear its honest fame,

Shall prove to a callous people
　　That the sense of a soldier's worth,
That the love of comrades, the honour of arms,
　　Have not yet perished from earth.

THE ADVANCE-GUARD.

In the dream of the Northern poets,
  The braves who in battle die
Fight on in shadowy phalanx
  In the field of the upper sky;
And as we read the sounding rhyme,
  The reverent fancy hears
The ghostly ring of the viewless swords
  And the clash of the spectral spears.

We think with imperious questionings
  Of the brothers whom we have lost,
And we strive to track in death's mystery
  The flight of each valiant ghost.
The Northern myth comes back to us,
  And we feel, through our sorrow's night,
That those young souls are striving still
  Somewhere for the truth and light.

It was not their time for rest and sleep;
  Their hearts beat high and strong;
In their fresh veins the blood of youth
  Was singing its hot, sweet song.
The open heaven bent over them,
  'Mid flowers their lithe feet trod,
Their lives lay vivid in light, and blest
  By the smiles of women and God.

Again they come!   Again I hear
  The tread of that goodly band;
I know the flash of Ellsworth's eye
  And the grasp of his hard, warm hand;
And Putnam, and Shaw, of the lion-heart,
  And an eye like a Boston girl's;
And I see the light of heaven which lay
  On Ulric Dahlgren's curls.

There is no power in the gloom of hell
  To quench those spirits' fire ;
There is no power in the bliss of heaven
  To bid them not aspire ;
But somewhere in the eternal plan
  That strength, that life survive,
And like the files on Lookout's crest,
  Above death's clouds they strive.

A chosen corps, they are marching on
  In a wider field than ours ;
Those bright battalions still fulfil
  The scheme of the heavenly powers ;
And high brave thoughts float down to us,
  The echoes of that far fight,
Like the flash of a distant picket's gun
  Through the shades of the severing night.

No fear for them ! In our lower field
  Let us keep our arms unstained,
That at last we be worthy to stand with them
  On the shining heights they've gained.
We shall meet and greet in closing ranks
  In Time's declining sun,
When the bugles of God shall sound recall
  And the battle of life be won.

LOVE'S PRAYER.

IF Heaven would hear my prayer,
　　My dearest wish would be,
Thy sorrows not to share,
　　But take them all on me ;
If Heaven would hear my prayer.

I'd beg with prayers and sighs
　　That never a tear might flow
From out thy lovely eyes,
　　If Heaven might grant it so ;
Mine be the tears and sighs.

No cloud thy brow should cover,
　　But smiles each other chase
From lips to eyes all over
　　Thy sweet and sunny face ;
The clouds my heart should cover.

That all thy path be light
　　Let darkness fall on me ;
If all thy days be bright,
　　Mine black as night could be.
My love would light my night.

For thou art more than life,
　　And if our fate should set
Life and my love at strife,
　　How could I then forget
I love thee more than life?

CHRISTINE.

THE beauty of the Northern dawns,
 Their pure, pale light is thine;
Yet all the dreams of tropic nights
 Within thy blue eyes shine.
Not statelier in their prisoning seas
 The icebergs grandly move,
But in thy smile is youth and joy,
 And in thy voice is love.

Thou art like Hecla's crest that stands
 So lonely, proud, and high,
No earthly thing may come between
 Her summit and the sky.
The sun in vain may strive to melt
 Her crown of virgin snow—
But the great heart of the mountain glows
 With deathless fire below.

EXPECTATION.

Roll on, O shining sun,
　　To the far seas !
Bring down, ye shades of eve,
　　The soft, salt breeze !
Shine out, O stars, and light
My darling's pathway bright,
As through the summer night
　　She comes to me.

No beam of any star
　　Can match her eyes ;
Her smile the bursting day
　　In light outvies.
Her voice—the sweetest thing
Heard by the raptured spring
When waking wild-woods ring—
　　She comes to me.

Ye stars, more swiftly wheel
　　O'er earth's still breast ;
More wildly plunge and reel
　　In the dim west !
The earth is lone and lorn,
Till the glad day be born,
Till with the happy morn
　　She comes to me.

TO FLORA.

WHEN April woke the drowsy flowers,
  And vagrant odours thronged the breeze,
And bluebirds wrangled in the bowers,
  And daisies flashed along the leas,
And faint arbutus strove among
  Dead winter's leaf-strewn wreck to rise,
And nature's sweetly jubilant song
  Went murmuring up the sunny skies,
Into this cheerful world you came,
And gained by right your vernal name.

I think the springs have changed of late,
  For " Arctics " are my daily wear,
The skies are turned to cold grey slate,
  And zephyrs are but draughts of air ;
But you make up whate'er we lack,
  When we, too rarely, come together,
More potent than the almanac,
  You bring the ideal April weather ;
When you are with us we defy
The blustering air, the lowering sky ;
In spite of winter's icy darts,
We've spring and sunshine in our hearts.

In fine, upon this April day,
  This deep conundrum I will bring :
Tell me the two good reasons, pray,
  I have, to say you are like spring ?

[You give it up ?] Because we love you—
  And see so very little of you.

A HAUNTED ROOM.

In the dim chamber whence but yesterday
  Passed my belovèd, filled with awe I stand ;
  And haunting Loves fluttering on every hand
Whisper her praises who is far away.
A thousand delicate fancies glance and play
  On every object which her robes have fanned,
  And tenderest thoughts and hopes bloom and
      expand
In the sweet memory of her beauty's ray.
Ah ! could that glass but hold the faintest trace
  Of all the loveliness once mirrored there,
  The clustering glory of the shadowy hair
That framed so well the dear young angel face !
  But no, it shows my own face, full of care,
And my heart is her beauty's dwelling-place.

DREAMS.

I LOVE a woman tenderly,
But cannot know if she loves me.
I press her hand, her lips I kiss,
But still love's full assurance miss.
Our waking life for ever seems
Cleft by a veil of doubt and dreams.

But love and night and sleep combine
In dreams to make her wholly mine.
A sure love lights her eyes' deep blue,
Her hands and lips are warm and true.
Always the fact unreal seems,
And truth I find alone in dreams.

THE LIGHT OF LOVE.

EACH shining light above us
    Has its own peculiar grace ;
But every light of heaven
    Is in my darling's face.

For it is like the sunlight,
    So strong and pure and warm,
That folds all good and happy things,
    And guards from gloom and harm.

And it is like the moonlight,
    So holy and so calm ;
The rapt peace of a summer night,
    When soft winds die in balm.

And it is like the starlight ;
  For, love her as I may,
She dwells still lofty and serene
  In mystery far away.

QUAND MÊME.

I STROVE, like Israel, with my youth,
  And said, " Till thou bestow
Upon my life Love's joy and truth,
  I will not let thee go."

And sudden on my night there woke
  The trouble of the dawn ;
Out of the east the red light broke,
  To broaden on and on.

And now let death be far or nigh,
  Let fortune gloom or shine,
I cannot all untimely die,
  For love, for love is mine.

My days are tuned to finer chords,
  And lit by higher suns ;
Through all my thoughts and all my words
  A purer purpose runs.

The blank page of my heart grows rife
  With wealth of tender lore ;
Her image, stamped upon my life,
  Gives value evermore.

She is so noble, firm, and true,
  I drink truth from her eyes,
As violets gain the heaven's own blue
  In gazing at the skies.

No matter if my hands attain
  The golden crown or cross ;
Only to love is such a gain
  That losing is not loss.

And thus whatever fate betide
  Of rapture or of pain,
If storm or sun the future hide,
  My love is not in vain.

So only thanks are on my lips ;
  And through my love I see
My earliest dreams, like freighted ships,
  Come sailing home to me.

WORDS.

WHEN violets were springing
  And sunshine filled the day,
And happy birds were singing
  The praises of the May,
A word came to me, blighting
  The beauty of the scene,
And in my heart was winter,
  Though all the trees were green.

Now down the blast go sailing
  The dead leaves, brown and sere ;
The forests are bewailing
  The dying of the year ;
A word comes to me, lighting
  With rapture all the air,
And in my heart is summer,
  Though all the trees are bare.

THE STIRRUP-CUP.

My short and happy day is done,
The long and dreary night comes on ;
And at my door the Pale Horse stands,
To carry me to unknown lands.

His whinny shrill, his pawing hoof,
Sound dreadful as a gathering storm ;
And I must leave this sheltering roof,
And joys of life so soft and warm.

Tender and warm the joys of life,—
Good friends, the faithful and the true ;
My rosy children and my wife,
So sweet to kiss, so fair to view.

So sweet to kiss, so fair to view,—
The night comes down, the lights burn blue ;
And at my door the Pale Horse stands,
To bear me forth to unknown lands.

A DREAM OF BRIC-A-BRAC.

[C. K. *loquitur*.]

I DREAMED I was in fair Niphon.
Amid tea-fields I journeyed on,
Reclined in my jinrikishaw;
Across the rolling plains I saw
The lordly Fusi-yama rise,
His blue cone lost in bluer skies.

At last I bade my bearers stop
Before what seemed a china-shop.
I roused myself and entered in.
A fearful joy, like some sweet sin,
Pierced through my bosom as I gazed,
Entranced, transported, and amazed.

For all the house was but one room,
And in its clear and grateful gloom,
Filled with all odours strange and strong
That to the wondrous East belong,
I saw above, around, below,
A sight to make the warm heart glow,
And leave the eager soul no lack,—
An endless wealth of bric-a-brac.

I saw bronze statues, old and rare,
Fashioned by no mere mortal skill,
With robes that fluttered in the air,
Blown out by Art's eternal will;
And delicate ivory netsukes,
Richer in tone than Cheddar cheese,
Of saints and hermits, cats and dogs,
Grim warriors and ecstatic frogs.

And here and there those wondrous masks,
More living flesh than sandal-wood,
Where the full soul in pleasure basks
And dreams of love, the only good.
The walls were all with pictures hung :
Gay villas bright in rain-washed air,
Trees to whose boughs brown monkeys clung,
Outlineless dabs of fuzzy hair.
And all about the opulent shelves
Littered with porcelain beyond price :
Imari pots arrayed themselves
Beside Ming dishes ; grain-of-rice
Vied with the Royal Satsuma,
Proud of its sallow ivory beam ;
And Kaga's Thousand Hermits lay
Tranced in some punch-bowl's golden gleam.
Over bronze censers, black with age,
The five-clawed dragons strife engage ;
A curled and insolent Dog of Foo
Sniffs at the smoke aspiring through.

In what old days, in what far lands,
What busy brains, what cunning hands,
With what quaint speech, what alien thought,
Strange fellow-men these marvels wrought !

As thus I mused, I was aware
There grew before my eager eyes
A little maid too bright and fair,
Too strangely lovely for surprise.
It seemed the beauty of the place
Had suddenly become concrete,
So full was she of Orient grace,
From her slant eyes and burnished face
Down to her little gold-bronzed feet.
She was a girl of old Japan ;
Her small hand held a gilded fan,
Which scattered fragrance through the room;
Her cheek was rich with pallid bloom,
Her eye was dark with languid fire,
Her red lips breathed a vague desire ;

Her teeth, of pearl inviolate,
Sweetly proclaimed her maiden state.
Her garb was stiff with broidered gold
Twined with mysterious fold on fold,
That gave no hint where, hidden well,
Her dainty form might warmly dwell,—
A pearl within too large a shell.
So quaint, so short, so lissome, she,
It seemed as if it well might be
Some jocose god, with sportive whirl,
Had taken up a long lithe girl
And tied a graceful knot in her.
I tried to speak, and found, oh, bliss !
I needed no interpreter ;
I knew the Japanese for kiss,—
I had no other thought but this ;
And she, with smile and blush divine,
Kind to my stammering prayer did seem ;
My thought was hers, and hers was mine,
In the swift logic of my dream.
My arms clung round her slender waist,
Through gold and silk the form I traced,
And glad as rain that follows drouth,
I kissed and kissed her bright red mouth.

What ailed the girl? No loving sigh
Heaved the round bosom ; in her eye
Trembled no tear ; from her dear throat
Bubbled a sweet and silvery note
Of girlish laughter, shrill and clear,
That all the statues seemed to hear.
The bronzes tinkled laughter fine ;
I heard a chuckle argentine
Ring from the silver images ;
Even the ivory netsukes
Uttered in every silent pause
Dry, bony laughs from tiny jaws ;
The painted monkeys on the wall
Waked up with chatter impudent ;
Pottery, porcelain, bronze, and all
Broke out in ghostly merriment,—

Faint as rain pattering on dry leaves,
Or cricket's chirp on summer eves.

And suddenly upon my sight
There grew a portent : left and right,
On every side, as if the air
Had taken substance then and there,
In every sort of form and face,
A throng of tourists filled the place.
I saw a Frenchman's sneering shrug ;
A German countess, in one hand
A sky-blue string which held a pug,
With the other a fiery face she fanned ;
A Yankee with a soft felt hat ;
A Coptic priest from Ararat ;
An English girl with cheeks of rose ;
A Nihilist with Socratic nose ;
Paddy from Cork with baggage light
And pockets stuffed with dynamite ;
A haughty Southern Readjuster,
Wrapped in his pride and linen duster ;
Two noisy New York stockbrokers,
And twenty British globe-trotters.
To my disgust and vast surprise,
They turned on me lack-lustre eyes,
And each with dropped and wagging jaw
Burst out into a wild guffaw :
They laughed with huge mouths opened wide ;
They roared till each one held his side ;
They screamed and writhed with brutal glee,
With fingers rudely stretched to me, —
Till lo ! at once the laughter died,
The tourists faded into air ;
None but my fair maid lingered there,
Who stood demurely by my side.
" Who were your friends ? " I asked the maid,
Taking a tea-cup from its shelf.
" This audience is disclosed," she said,
" Whenever a man makes a fool of himself."

LIBERTY.

WHAT man is there so bold that he should say,
"Thus, and thus only, would I have the sea"?
For whether lying calm and beautiful,
Clasping the earth in love, and throwing back
The smile of heaven from waves of amethyst ;
Or whether, freshened by the busy winds,
It bears the trade and navies of the world
To ends of use or stern activity ;
Or whether, lashed by tempests, it gives way
To elemental fury, howls and roars
At all its rocky barriers, in wild lust
Of ruin drinks the blood of living things,
And strews its wrecks o'er leagues of desolate
　　shore,—
Always it is the sea, and men bow down
Before its vast and varied majesty.

So all in vain will timorous ones essay
To set the metes and bounds of Liberty.
For Freedom is its own eternal law ;
It makes its own conditions, and in storm
Or calm alike fulfils the unerring Will.
Let us not then despise it when it lies
Still as a sleeping lion, while a swarm
Of gnat-like evils hover round its head ;
Nor doubt it when in mad, disjointed times
It shakes the torch of terror, and its cry
Shrills o'er the quaking earth, and in the flame
Of riot and war we see its awful form
Rise by the scaffold, where the crimson axe
Rings down its grooves the knell of shuddering
　　kings.
For ever in thine eyes, O Liberty,
Shines that high light whereby the world is saved,
And though thou slay us, we will trust in thee !

THE WHITE FLAG.

I SENT my love two roses,—one
    As white as driven snow,
And one a blushing royal red,
    A flaming Jacqueminot.

I meant to touch and test my fate ;
    That night I should divine,
The moment I should see my love,
    If her true heart were mine.

For if she holds me dear, I said,
    She'll wear my blushing rose ;
If not, she'll wear my cold Lamarque
    As white as winter's snows.

My heart sank when I met her : sure
    I had been over bold,
For on her breast my pale rose lay
    In virgin whiteness cold.

Yet with low words she greeted me,
    With smiles divinely tender ;
Upon her cheek the red rose dawned,—
    The white rose meant surrender.

THE LAW OF DEATH.

THE song of Kilvani : fairest she
In all the land of Savatthi.
She had one child, as sweet and gay
And dear to her as the light of day.
She was so young, and he so fair,
The same bright eyes and the same dark hair ;
To see them by the blossomy way,
They seemed two children at their play.

There came a death-dart from the sky,
Kilvani saw her darling die.
The glimmering shade his eyes invades,
Out of his cheek the red bloom fades ;
His warm heart feels the icy chill,
The round limbs shudder, and are still.
And yet Kilvani held him fast
Long after life's last pulse was past,
As if her kisses could restore
The smile gone out for evermore.

But when she saw her child was dead,
She scattered ashes on her head,
And seized the small corpse, pale and sweet,
And rushing wildly through the street,
She sobbing fell at Buddha's feet.

"Master, all-helpful, help me now !
Here at thy feet I humbly bow ;
Have mercy, Buddha, help me now !"
She grovelled on the marble floor,
And kissed the dead child o'er and o'er.
And suddenly upon the air
There fell the answer to her prayer :
" Bring me to-night a lotus tied
With thread from a house where none has died."

She rose, and laughed with thankful joy,
Sure that the god would save the boy.
She found a lotus by the stream ;
She plucked it from its noonday dream,
And then from door to door she fared,
To ask what house by Death was spared.
Her heart grew cold to see the eyes
Of all dilate with slow surprise :
" Kilvani, thou hast lost thy head ;
Nothing can help a child that's dead.
There stands not by the Ganges' side
A house where none hath ever died."
Thus, through the long and weary day,
From every door she bore away
Within her heart, and on her arm,
A heavier load, a deeper harm.
By gates of gold and ivory,
By wattled huts of poverty,
The same refrain heard poor Kilvani,
The living are few, the dead are many.

The evening came—so still and fleet—
And overtook her hurrying feet.
And, heartsick, by the sacred fane
She fell, and prayed the god again.
She sobbed and beat her bursting breast :
" Ah, thou hast mocked me, Mightiest !
Lo ! I have wandered far and wide ;
There stands no house where none hath died."
And Buddha answered, in a tone
Soft as a flute at twilight blown,
But grand as heaven and strong as death
To him who hears with ears of faith :
" Child, thou art answered.   Murmur not !
Bow, and accept the common lot."

Kilvani heard with reverence meet,
And laid her child at Buddha's feet.

MOUNT TABOR.

On Tabor's height a glory came,
And, shrined in clouds of lambent flame,
The awestruck, hushed disciples saw
Christ and the prophets of the law.
Moses, whose grand and awful face
Of Sinai's thunder bore the trace,
And wise Elias,—in his eyes
The shade of Israel's prophecies,—
Stood in that wide, mysterious light,
Than Syrian noons more purely bright,
One on each hand, and high between
Shone forth the godlike Nazarene.
They bowed their heads in holy fright,—
No mortal eyes could bear the sight,—
And when they looked again, behold !
The fiery clouds had backward rolled,
And borne aloft in grandeur lonely,
Nothing was left " save Jesus only."

Resplendent type of things to be !
We read its mystery to-day
With clearer eyes than even they,
The fisher-saints of Galilee.
We see the Christ stand out between
The ancient law and faith serene,
Spirit and letter ; but above
Spirit and letter both was Love.
Led by the hand of Jacob's God,
Through wastes of eld a path was trod
By which the savage world could move
Upward through law and faith to love.
And there in Tabor's harmless flame
The crowning revelation came.

The old world knelt in homage due,
The prophets near in reverence drew,
Law ceased its mission to fulfil,
And Love was lord on Tabor's hill.

So now, while creeds perplex the mind
And wranglings load the weary wind,
When all the air is filled with words
And texts that wring like clashing swords,
Still, as for refuge, we may turn
Where Tabor's shining glories burn,—
The soul of antique Israel gone,
And nothing left but Christ alone.

RELIGION AND DOCTRINE.

HE stood before the Sanhedrim;
The scowling rabbis gazed at him.
He recked not of their praise or blame;
There was no fear, there was no shame,
For one upon whose dazzled eyes
The whole world poured its vast surprise.
The open heaven was far too near,
His first day's light too sweet and clear,
To let him waste his new-gained ken
On the hate-clouded face of men.

But still they questioned, "Who art thou?
What hast thou been? What art thou now?
Thou art not he who yesterday
Sat here and begged beside the way;
For he was blind."
      —"*And I am he;*
For I was blind, but now I see."

He told the story o'er and o'er ;
It was his full heart's only lore :
A prophet on the Sabbath-day
Had touched his sightless eyes with clay,
And made him see who had been blind.
Their words passed by him like the wind,
Which raves and howls, but cannot shock
The hundred-fathom-rooted rock.

Their threats and fury all went wide ;
They could not touch his Hebrew pride.
Their sneers at Jesus and His band,
Nameless and homeless in the land,
Their boasts of Moses and his Lord,
All could not change him by one word.

" I know not what this man may be,
Sinner or saint ; but as for me,
One thing I know,—that I am he
Who once was blind, and now I see."

They were all doctors of renown,
The great men of a famous town,
With deep brows, wrinkled, broad, and wise,
Beneath their wide phylacteries ;
The wisdom of the East was theirs,
And honour crowned their silver hairs.
The man they jeered and laughed to scorn
Was unlearned, poor, and humbly born ;
But he knew better far than they
What came to him that Sabbath-day ;
And what the Christ had done for him
He knew, and not the Sanhedrim.

SINAI AND CALVARY.

There are two mountains hallowed
    By majesty sublime,
Which rear their crests unconquered
    Above the floods of Time.
Uncounted generations
    Have gazed on them with awe,—
The mountain of the Gospel,
    The mountain of the Law.

From Sinai's cloud of darkness
    The vivid lightnings play ;
They serve the God of vengeance,
    The Lord who shall repay.
Each fault must bring its penance,
    Each sin the avenging blade,
For God upholds in justice
    The laws that He hath made.

But Calvary stands to ransom
    The earth from utter loss,
In shade than light more glorious,
    The shadow of the Cross.
To heal a sick world's trouble,
    To soothe its woe and pain,
On Calvary's sacred summit
    The Paschal Lamb was slain.

The boundless might of Heaven
    Its law in mercy furled,
As once the bow of promise
    O'erarched a drowning world.

The Law said, "As you keep me,
　　It shall be done to you;"
But Calvary prays, "Forgive them;
　　They know not what they do."

Almighty God! direct us
　　To keep Thy perfect Law!
O blessed Saviour, help us
　　Nearer to Thee to draw!
Let Sinai's thunders aid us
　　To guard our feet from sin;
And Calvary's light inspire us
　　The love of God to win.

THE VISION OF ST. PETER.

To Peter by night the faithfullest came
　　And said, "We appeal to thee!
The life of the Church is in thy life;
　　We pray thee to rise and flee.

"For the tyrant's hand is red with blood,
　　And his arm is heavy with power;
Thy head, the head of the Church, will fall
　　If thou tarry in Rome an hour."

Through the sleeping town St. Peter passed
　　To the wide Campagna plain;
In the starry light of the Alban night
　　He drew free breath again:

When across his path an awful form
　　In luminous glory stood;
His thorn-crowned brow, His hands and feet,
　　Were wet with immortal blood.

The godlike sorrow which filled His eyes
    Seemed changed to a godlike wrath
As they turned on Peter, who cried aloud,
    And sank to his knees in the path.

"Lord of my life, my love, my soul!
    Say, what wilt Thou with me?"
A voice replied, "I go to Rome
    To be crucified for thee."

The Apostle sprang, all flushed, to his feet,—
    The vision had passed away;
The light still lay on the dewy plain,
    But the sky in the east was gray.

To the city walls St. Peter turned,
    And his heart in his breast grew fire;
In every vein the hot blood burned
    With the strength of one high desire.

And sturdily back he marched to his death
    Of terrible pain and shame;
And never a shade of fear again
    To the stout Apostle came.

ISRAEL.

WHEN by Jabbok the patriarch waited
  To learn on the morrow his doom,
And his dubious spirit debated
  In darkness and silence and gloom,
  There descended a Being with whom
He wrestled in agony sore,
  With striving of heart and of brawn,
And not for an instant forbore
  Till the east gave a threat of the dawn ;
And then, as the Awful One blessed him,
  To his lips and his spirit there came,
Compelled by the doubts that oppressed him,
The cry that through questioning ages
Has been wrung from the hinds and the sages,
  "Tell me, I pray Thee, Thy name !"

Most fatal, most futile, of questions !
  Wherever the heart of man beats,
  In the spirit's most sacred retreats,
It comes with its sombre suggestions,
  Unanswered for ever and aye.
  The blessing may come and may stay,
For the wrestler's heroic endeavour ;
But the question, unheeded for ever,
  Dies out in the broadening day.

In the ages before our traditions,
By the altars of dark superstitions,
  The imperious question has come ;
When the death-stricken victim lay sobbing
  At the feet of his slayer and priest,
And his heart was laid smoking and throbbing
  To the sound of the cymbal and drum

On the steps of the high Teocallis;
  When the delicate Greek at his feast
Poured forth the red wine from his chalice
  With mocking and cynical prayer;
When by Nile Egypt worshipping lay,
  And afar, through the rosy, flushed air
The Memnon called out to the day;
Where the Muezzin's cry floats from his spire;
  In the vaulted Cathedral's dim shades,
Where the crushed hearts of thousands aspire
Through art's highest miracles higher,
  This question of question's invades
  Each heart bowed in worship or shame;
In the air where the censers are swinging,
A voice, going up with the singing,
  Cries, "Tell me, I pray Thee, Thy name!"

No answer came back, not a word,
To the patriarch there by the ford;
No answer has come through the ages
To the poets, the seers, and the sages
Who have sought in the secrets of science
The name and the nature of God,
Whether cursing in desperate defiance
Or kissing His absolute rod;
But the answer which was and shall be,
"My name! Nay, what is it to thee?"
The search and the question are vain.
By use of the strength that is in you,
By wrestling of soul and of sinew
The blessing of God you may gain.

There are lights in the far-gleaming Heaven
  That never will shine on our eyes;
To mortals it may not be given
  To range those inviolate skies.
The mind, whether praying or scorning,
  That tempts those dread secrets shall fail;
But strive through the night till the morning,
  Aud mightily shalt thou prevail.

THE CROWS AT WASHINGTON.

SLOW flapping to the setting sun
  By twos and threes, in wavering rows,
  As twilight shadows dimly close,
The crows fly over Washington.

Under the crimson sunset sky
Virginian woodlands leafless lie,
  In wintry torpor bleak and dun.
Through the rich vault of heaven, which shines.
  Like a warmed opal in the sun,
With wide advance in broken lines
  The crows fly over Washington.

Over the Capitol's white dome,
  Across the obelisk soaring bare
To prick the clouds, they travel home,
Content and weary, winnowing
  With dusky vans the golden air,
Which hints the coming of the spring,
  Though winter whitens Washington.

The dim, deep air, the level ray
Of dying sunlight on their plumes,
  Give them a beauty not their own ;
Their hoarse notes fail and faint away ;
  A rustling murmur floating down
Blends sweetly with the thickening glooms ;
They touch with grace the fading day,
  Slow flying over Washington.

I stand and watch with clouded eyes
  These dim battalions move along ;
Out of the distance memory cries
  Of days when life and hope were strong,

When love was prompt and wit was gay ;
Even then, at evening, as to-day,
  I watched, while twilight hovered dim
  Over Potomac's curving rim,
This selfsame flight of homing crows
Blotting the sunset's fading rose,
  Above the roofs of Washington.

REMORSE.

SAD is the thought of sunniest days
  Of love and rapture perished,
And shine through memory's tearful haze
  The eyes once fondliest cherished.
Reproachful is the ghost of toys
  That charmed while life was wasted.
But saddest is the thought of joys
  That never yet were tasted.

Sad is the vague and tender dream
  Of dead love's lingering kisses,
To crushed hearts haloed by the gleam
  Of unreturning blisses ;
Deep mourns the soul in anguished pride
  For the pitiless death that won them,—
But the saddest wail is for lips that died
  With the virgin dew upon them.

ESSE QUAM VIDERI.

THE knightly legend of thy shield betrays
   The moral of thy life ; a forecast wise,
   And that large honour that deceit defies,
Inspired thy fathers in the elder days,
Who decked thy scutcheon with that sturdy phrase,
   To be rather than seem. As eve's red skies
   Surpass the morning's rosy prophecies,
Thy life to that proud boast its answer pays.
Scorning thy faith and purpose to defend
   The ever-mutable multitude at last
   Will hail the power they did not comprehend,—
Thy fame will broaden through the centuries ;
   As, storm and billowy tumult overpast,
   The moon rules calmly o'er the conquered seas.

WHEN THE BOYS COME HOME.

THERE'S a happy time coming,
   When the boys come home.
There's a glorious day coming,
   When the boys come home.
We will end the dreadful story
Of this treason dark and gory
In a sunburst of glory,
   When the boys come home.

The day will seem brighter
   When the boys come home,
For our hearts will be lighter
   When the boys come home.
Wives and sweethearts will press them
In their arms and caress them,
And pray God to bless them,
   When the boys come home.

The thinned ranks will be proudest
   When the boys come home,
And their cheer will ring the loudest
   When the boys come home.
The full ranks will be shattered,
And the bright arms will be battered,
And the battle-standards tattered,
   When the boys come home.

Their bayonets may be rusty,
   When the boys come home,
And their uniforms dusty,
   When the boys come home.
But all shall see the traces
Of battle's royal graces,
In the brown and bearded faces,
   When the boys come home.

Our love shall go to meet them,
  When the boys come home,
To bless them and to greet them,
  When the boys come home ;
And the fame of their endeavour
Time and change shall not dissever
From the nation's heart for ever,
  When the boys come home.

LÈSE-AMOUR.

How well my heart remembers
Beside these camp-fire embers
The eyes that smiled so far away,—
The joy that was November's.

Her voice to laughter moving,
So merrily reproving,—
We wandered through the autumn woods,
And neither thought of loving.

The hills with light were glowing,
The waves in joy were flowing,—
It was not to the clouded sun
The day's delight was owing.

Though through the brown leaves straying,
Our lives seemed gone a-Maying ;
We knew not Love was with us there,
No look nor tone betraying.

How unbelief still misses
The best of being's blisses !
Our parting saw the first and last
Of love's imagined kisses.

Now 'mid these scenes the drearest
I dream of her, the dearest,—
Whose eyes outshine the Southern stars,
So far, and yet the nearest.

And Love, so gaily taunted,
Who died, no welcome granted,
Comes to me now, a pallid ghost,
By whom my life is haunted.

With bonds I may not sever,
He binds my heart for ever,
And leads me where we murdered him,—
The Hill beside the River.

CAMP SHAW, FLORIDA,
February 1864.

—⊶⊷—

NORTHWARD.

UNDER the high unclouded sun
That makes the ship and shadow one,
I sail away as from the fort
Booms sullenly the noonday gun.

The odorous airs blow thin and fine,
The sparkling waves like emeralds shine,
The lustre of the coral reefs
Gleams whitely through the tepid brine.

And glitters o'er the liquid miles
The jewelled ring of verdant isles,
Where generous Nature holds her court
Of ripened bloom and sunny smiles.

Encinctured by the faithful seas
Inviolate gardens load the breeze,
　　Where flaunt like giant-warders' plumes
The pennants of the cocoa-trees.

Enthroned in light and bathed in balm,
In lonely majesty the Palm
　　Blesses the isles with waving hands,—
High-Priest of the eternal Calm.

Yet Northward with an equal mind
I steer my course, and leave behind
　　The rapture of the Southern skies,—
The wooing of the Southern wind.

For here o'er Nature's wanton bloom
Falls far and near the shade of gloom,
　　Cast from the hovering vulture-wings
Of one dark thought of woe and doom.

I know that in the snow-white pines
The brave Norse fire of freedom shines,
　　And fain for this I leave the land
Where endless summer pranks the vines.

O strong, free North, so wise and brave!
O South, too lovely for a slave!
　　Why read ye not the changeless truth,—
The free can conquer but to save?

May God upon these shining sands
Send Love and Victory clasping hands,
　　And Freedom's banners wave in peace
For ever o'er the rescued lands!

And here, in that triumphant hour,
Shall yielding beauty wed with power;
　　And blushing earth and smiling sea
In dalliance deck the bridal bower.

Key West, 1864.

IN THE FIRELIGHT.

MY dear wife sits beside the fire
   With folded hands and dreaming eyes,
Watching the restless flames aspire,
   And rapt in thralling memories.
I mark the fitful firelight fling
   Its warm caresses on her brow,
   And kiss her hands' unmelting snow,
And glisten on her wedding-ring.

The proud free head that crowns so well
   The neck superb, whose outlines glide
Into the bosom's perfect swell
   Soft-billowed by its peaceful tide,
The cheek's faint flush, the lip's red glow,
   The gracious charm her beauty wears,
   Fill my fond eyes with tender tears
As in the days of long ago.

Days long ago, when in her eyes
   The only heaven I cared for lay,
When from our thoughtless Paradise
   All care and toil dwelt far away ;
When Hope in wayward fancies throve,
   And rioted in secret sweets,
   Beguiled by Passion's dear deceits,—
The mysteries of maiden love.

One year had passed since first my sight
   Was gladdened by her girlish charms,
When on a rapturous summer night
   I clasped her in possessing arms.
And now ten years have rolled away,
   And left such blessings as their dower ;
   I owe her tenfold at this hour
The love that lit our wedding-day.

For now, vague-hovering o'er her form,
  My fancy sees, by love refined,
A warmer and a dearer charm
  By wedlock's mystic hands entwined,—
A golden coil of wifely cares
  That years have forged, the loving joy
  That guards the curly-headed boy
Asleep an hour ago upstairs.

A fair young mother, pure as fair,
  A matron heart and virgin soul!
The flickering light that crowns her hair
  Seems like a saintly aureole.
A tender sense upon me falls
  That joy unmerited is mine,
  And in this pleasant twilight shine
My perfect bliss myself appals.

Come back! my darling, strayed so far
  Into the realm of fantasy,—
Let thy dear face shine like a star
  In love-light beaming over me.
My melting soul is jealous, sweet,
  Of thy long silence' drear eclipse;
  O kiss me back with living lips,
To life, love, lying at thy feet!

IN A GRAVEYARD.

IN the dewy depths of the graveyard
   I lie in the tangled grass,
And watch, in the sea of azure,
   The white cloud-islands pass.

The birds in the rustling branches
   Sing gaily overhead ;
Grey stones like sentinel spectres
   Are guarding the silent dead.

The early flowers sleep shaded
   In the cool green noonday glooms ;
The broken light falls shuddering
   On the cold white face of the tombs.

Without, the world is smiling
   In the infinite love of God,
But the sunlight fails and falters
   When it falls on the churchyard sod.

On me the joyous rapture
   Of a heart's first love is shed,
But it falls on my heart as coldly
   As sunlight on the dead.

THE PRAIRIE.

THE skies are blue above my head,
  The prairie green below,
And flickering o'er the tufted grass
  The shifting shadows go,
Vague-sailing, where the feathery clouds
  Fleck white the tranquil skies,
Black javelins darting where aloft
  The whirring pheasant flies.

A glimmering plain in drowsy trance
  The dim horizon bounds,
Where all the air is resonant
  With sleepy summer sounds,—
The life that sings among the flowers,
  The lisping of the breeze,
The hot cicala's sultry cry,
  The murmurous dream of bees.

The butterfly—a flying flower—
  Wheels swift in flashing rings,
And flutters round his quiet kin,
  With brave flame-mottled wings.
The wild Pinks burst in crimson fire
  The Phlox' bright clusters shine,
And Prairie-Cups are swinging free
  To spill their airy wine.

And lavishly beneath the sun,
  In liberal splendour rolled,
The Fennel fills the dipping plain
  With floods of flowery gold ;

And widely weaves the Iron-Weed
A woof of purple dyes
Where Autumn's royal feet may tread
When bankrupt Summer flies.

In verdurous tumult far away
The prairie-billows gleam,
Upon their crests in blessing rests
The noontide's gracious beam.
Low quivering vapours steaming dim
The level splendours break
Where languid Lilies deck the rim
Of some land-circled lake.

Far in the east like low-hung clouds
The waving woodlands lie ;
Far in the west the glowing plain
.   Melts warmly in the sky.
No accent wounds the reverent air,
No footprint dints the sod,
Lone in the light the prairie lies
Rapt in a dream of God.

Illinois, 1858.

—————

CENTENNIAL.

A hundred times the bells of Brown
Have rung to sleep the idle summers,
And still to-day clangs clamouring down
A greeting to the welcome comers.

And far, like waves of morning, pours
Her call, in airy ripples breaking,
And wanders to the farthest shores,
Her children's drowsy hearts awaking.

The wild vibration floats along,
  O'er heart-strings tense its magic plying,
And wakes in every breast its song
  Of love and gratitude undying.

My heart to meet the summons leaps
  At limit of its straining tether,
Where the fresh western sunlight steeps
  In golden flame the prairie heather.

And others, happier, rise and fare
  To pass within the hallowed portal,
And see the glory shining there
  Shrined in her steadfast eyes immortal.

What though their eyes be dim and dull,
  Their heads be white in reverend blossom;
Our mother's smile is beautiful
  As when she bore them on her bosom!

Her heavenly forehead bears no line
  Of Time's iconolastic fingers,
But o'er her form the grace divine
  Of deathless youth and wisdom lingers.

We fade and pass, grow faint and old,
  Till youth and joy and hope are banished,
And still her beauty seems to fold
  The sum of all the glory vanished.

As while Tithonus faltered on
  The threshold of the Olympian dawnings,
Aurora's front eternal shone
  With lustre of the myriad mornings.

So joys that slip like dead leaves down,
  And hopes burnt out that die in ashes,
Rise restless from their graves to crown
  Our mother's brow with fadeless flashes.

And lives wrapped in tradition's mist
   These honoured halls to-day are haunting,
And lips by lips long withered kissed
   The sagas of the past are chanting.

Scornful of absence' envious bar
   BROWN smiles upon the mystic meeting
Of those her sons, who, sundered far,
   In brotherhood of heart are greeting;

Her wayward children wandering on
   Where setting stars are lowly burning,
But still in worship toward the dawn
   That gilds their souls' dear Mecca turning;

Or those who, armed for God's own fight,
   Stand by His Word through fire and slaughter,
Or bear our banner's starry light
   Far-flashing through the Gulf's blue water.

For where one strikes for light and truth,
   The right to aid, the wrong redressing,
The mother of his spirit's youth
   Sheds o'er his soul her silent blessing.

She gained her crown a gem of flame
   When KNEASS fell dead in victory gory;
New splendour blazed upon her name
   When IVES' young life went out in glory!

Thus bright for ever may she keep
   Her fires of tolerant Freedom burning,
Till War's red eyes are charmed to sleep
   And bells ring home the boys returning.

And may she shed her radiant truth
   In largess on ingenuous comers,
And hold the bloom of gracious youth
   Through many a hundred tranquil summers!

A WINTER NIGHT.

THE winter wind is raving fierce and shrill,
   And chides with angry moan the frosty skies;
   The white stars gaze with sleepless Gorgon eyes
That freeze the earth in terror fixed and still.
We reck not of the wild night's gloom and chill,
   Housed from its rage, dear friend; and fancy flies,
   Lured by the hand of beckoning memories,
Back to those summer evenings on the hill
Where we together watched the sun go down
   Beyond the gold-washed uplands, while his fires
   Touched into glittering life the vanes and spires
Piercing the purpling mists that veiled the town.
   The wintry night thy voice and eyes beguile,
   Till wake the sleeping summers in thy smile.

STUDENT-SONG.

WHEN Youth's warm heart beats high, my friend,
  And Youth's blue sky is bright,
And shines in Youth's clear eye, my friend,
  Love's early dawning light,
Let the free soul spurn care's control,
  And while the glad days shine,
We'll use their beams for Youth's gay dreams
  Of Love and Song and Wine.

Let not the bigot's frown, my friend,
  O'ercast thy brow with gloom,
For Autumn's sober brown, my friend,
  Shall follow Summer's bloom.
Let smiles and sighs and loving eyes
  In changeful beauty shine,
And shed their beams on Youth's gay dreams
  Of Love and Song and Wine.

For in the weary years, my friend,
  That stretched before us lie,
There'll be enough of tears, my friend,
  To dim the brightest eye.
So let them wait, and laugh at fate,
  While Youth's sweet moments shine,—
Till memory gleams with golden dreams
  Of Love and Song and Wine.

HOW IT HAPPENED.

I PRAY you, pardon me, Elsie,
    And smile that frown away
That dims the light of your lovely face
    As a thunder-cloud the day.
I really could not help it,—
    Before I thought, 'twas done,—
And those great grey eyes flashed bright and cold,
    Like an icicle in the sun.

I was thinking of the summers
    When we were boys and girls,
And wandered in the blossoming woods,
    And the gay winds romped with your curls.
And you seemed to me the same little girl
    I kissed in the alder-path,
I kissed the little girl's lips, and, alas!
    I have roused a woman's wrath.

There is not so much to pardon,—
    For why were your lips so red?
The blond hair fell in a shower of gold
    From the proud, provoking head.
And the beauty that flashed from the splendid eyes,
    And played round the tender mouth,
Rushed over my soul like a warm sweet wind
    That blows from the fragrant south.

And where, after all, is the harm done?
    I believe we were made to be gay,
And all of youth not given to love
    Is vainly squandered away.

And strewn through life's low labours,
  Like gold in the desert sands,
Are love's swift kisses and sighs and vows
  And the clasp of clinging hands.

And when you are old and lonely,
  In Memory's magic shine
You will see on your thin and wasting hands,
  Like gems, these kisses of mine.
And when you muse at evening
  At the sound of some vanished name,
The ghost of my kisses shall touch your lips
  And kindle your heart to flame.

GOD'S VENGEANCE.

SAITH the Lord, "Vengeance is mine;
  I will repay," saith the Lord;
Ours be the anger divine,
  Lit by the flash of His word.

How shall His vengeance be done?
  How, when His purpose is clear?
Must He come down from His throne?
  Hath He no instruments here?

Sleep not in imbecile trust,
  Waiting for God to begin,
While, growing strong in the dust,
  Rests the bruised serpent of sin.

Right and Wrong,—both cannot live
  Death-grappled. Which shall we see?
Strike ! only Justice can give
  Safety to all that shall be.

Shame ! to stand paltering thus,
    Tricked by the balancing odds ;
Strike ! God is waiting for us !
    Strike ! for the vengeance is God's.

—⁙—

TOO LATE.

HAD we but met in other days,
Had we but loved in other ways,
Another light and hope had shone
    On your life and my own.

In sweet but hopeless reveries
I fancy how your wistful eyes
Had saved me, had I known their power
    In fate's imperious hour ;

How loving you, beloved of God,
And following you, the path I trod
Had led me, through your love and prayers,
    To God's love unawares :

And how our beings joined as one
Had passed through checkered shade and sun,
Until the earth our lives had given,
    With little change, to heaven.

God knows why this was not to be.
You bloomed from childhood far from me.
The sunshine of the favoured place
    That knew your youth and grace.

And when your eyes, so fair and free,
In fearless beauty beamed on me,
I knew the fatal die was thrown,
    My choice in life was gone.

And still with wild and tender art
Your child-love touched my torpid heart,
Gilding the blackness where it fell,
    Like sunlight over hell.

In vain, in vain ! my choice was gone !
Better to struggle on alone
Than blot your pure life's blameless shine
    With cloudy stains of mine.

A vague regret, a troubled prayer,
And then the future vast and fair
Will tempt your young and eager eyes
    With all its glad surprise.

And I shall watch you, safe and far,
As some late traveller eyes a star
Wheeling beyond his desert sands
    To gladden happier lands.

E

LOVE'S DOUBT.

'Tis love that blinds my heart and eyes,—
  I sometimes say in doubting dreams,—
  The face that near me perfect seems
Cold Memory paints in fainter dyes.

'Twas but love's dazzled eyes—I say—
  That made her seem so strangely bright;
  The face I worshipped yesternight,
I dread to meet it changed to-day.

As, when dies out some song's refrain,
  And leaves your eyes in happy tears,
  Awake the same fond idle fears,—
It cannot sound so sweet again.

You wait and say with vague annoy,
  " It will not sound so sweet again,"
  Until comes back the wild refrain
That floods your soul with treble joy.

So when I see my love again
  Fades the unquiet doubt away,
  While shines her beauty like the day
Over my happy heart and brain.

And in that face I see no more
  The fancied faults I idly dreamed,
  But all the charms that fairest seemed,
I find them, fairer than before.

LAGRIMAS.

GOD send me tears !
Loose the fierce band that binds my tired brain,
Give me the melting heart of other years,
And let me weep again !

Before me pass
The shapes of things inexorably true.
Gone is the sparkle of transforming dew
From every blade of grass.

In life's high noon
Aimless I stand, my promised task undone,
And raise my hot eyes to the angry sun
That will go down too soon.

Turned into gall
Are the sweet joys of childhood's sunny reign;
And memory is a torture, love a chain
That binds my life in thrall.

And childhood's pain
Could to me now the purest rapture yield ;
I pray for tears as in his parching field
The husbandman for rain.

We pray in vain !
The sullen sky flings down its blaze of brass ;
The joys of life all scorched and withering pass ;
I shall not weep again.

ON THE BLUFF.

O GRANDLY flowing River!
O silver-gliding River!
Thy springing willows shiver
   In the sunset as of old;
They shiver in the silence
Of the willow-whitened islands,
While the sun-bars and the sand-bars
   Fill air and wave with gold.

O gay, oblivious River!
O sunset-kindled River!
Do you remember ever
   The eyes and skies so blue
On a summer day that shone here,
When we were all alone here,
And the blue eyes were too wise
   To speak the love they knew?

O stern, impassive River!
O still, unanswering River!
The shivering willows quiver
   As the night-winds moan and rave.
From the past a voice is calling,
From heaven a star is falling,
And dew swells in the bluebells
   Above her hillside grave.

UNA.

In the whole wide world there was but one ;
Others for others, but she was mine,
The one fair woman beneath the sun.

From her gold-flax curls' most marvellous shine
Down to the lithe and delicate feet
There was not a curve nor a waving line

But moved in a harmony firm and sweet
With all of passion my life could know.
By knowledge perfect and faith complete

I was bound to her,—as the planets go
Adoring around their central star,
Free, but united for weal or woe.

She was so near and Heaven so far—
She grew my heaven and law and fate,
Rounding my life with a mystic bar .

No thought beyond could violate.
Our love to fulness in silence nursed
Grew calm as morning, when through the gate

Of the glimmering east the sun has burst,
With his hot life filling the waiting air.
She kissed me once,—that last and first

Of her maiden kisses was placid as prayer.
Against all comers I sat with lance
In rest, and, drunk with my joy, I sware

Defiance and scorn to the world's worst chance.
In vain ! for soon unhorsed I lay
At the feet of the strong god Circumstance—

And never again shall break the day,
And never again shall fall the night,
That shall light me, or shield me, on my way

To the presence of my sad soul's delight.
Her dead love comes like a passionate ghost
To mourn the Body it held so light,

And Fate, like a hound with a purpose lost,
Goes round bewildered with shame and fright.

THROUGH THE LONG DAYS.

THROUGH the long days and years
What will my loved one be,
Parted from me?
Through the long days and years.

Always as then she was,
Loveliest, brightest, best,
Blessing and blest,—
Always as then she was.

Never on earth again
Shall I before her stand,
Touch lip or hand,—
Never on earth again.

But while my darling lives
Peaceful I journey on,
Not quite alone,
Not while my darling lives.

A PHYLACTERY.

Wise men I hold those rakes of old
   Who, as we read in antique story,
When lyres were struck and wine was poured,
Set the white Death's Head on the board—
     Memento mori.

Love well ! love truly ! and love fast !
   True love evades the dilatory.
Life's bloom flares like a meteor past ;
A joy so dazzling cannot last—
     Memento mori.

Stop not to pluck the leaves of bay
   That greenly deck the path of glory,
The wreath will wither if you stay,
So pass along your earnest way—
     Memento mori.

Hear but not heed, though wild and shrill,
   The cries of faction transitory ;
Cleave to *your* good, eschew *your* ill,
A Hundred Years and all is still—
     Memento mori.

When Old Age comes with muffled drums,
   That beat to sleep our tired life's story,
On thoughts of dying (Rest is good !),
Like old snakes coiled i' the sun, we brood—
     Memento mori.

BLONDINE.

I WANDERED through a careless world
 Deceived when not deceiving,
And never gave an idle heart
 The rapture of believing.
The smiles, the sighs, the glancing eyes,
 Of many hundred comers
Swept by me, light as rose-leaves blown
 From long-forgotten summers.

But never eyes so deep and bright
 And loyal in their seeming,
And never smiles so full of light
 Have shone upon my dreaming.
The looks and lips so gay and wise,
 The thousand charms that wreathe them,
—Almost I dare believe that truth
 Is safely shrined beneath them.

Ah ! do they shine, those eyes of thine,
 But for our own misleading?
The fresh young smile, so pure and fine,
 Does it but mock our reading?
Then faith is fled, and trust is dead,
 And unbelief grows duty,
If fraud can wield the triple arm
 Of youth and wit and beauty.

DISTICHES.

I.

WISELY a woman prefers to a lover a man who
neglects her.
This one may love her some day, some day the
lover will not.

II.

There are three species of creatures who when
they seem coming are going,
When they seem going they come : Diplomates,
women, and crabs.

III.

Pleasures too hastily tasted grow sweeter in fond
recollection,
As the pomegranate plucked green ripens far
over the sea.

IV.

As the meek beasts in the Garden came flocking
for Adam to name them,
Men for a title to-day crawl to the feet of a
king.

V.

What is a first love worth, except to prepare for
a second?
What does the second love bring? Only regret
for the first.

VI.

Health was wooed by the Romans in groves of
the laurel and myrtle.
Happy and long are the lives brightened by
glory and love.

VII.

Wine is like rain: when it falls on the mire it but
makes it the fouler,
But when it strikes the good soil wakes it to
beauty and bloom.

VIII.

Break not the rose ; its fragrance and beauty are
surely sufficient :
Resting contented with these, never a thorn
shall you feel.

IX.

When you break up housekeeping, you learn the
extent of your treasures ;
Till he begins to reform, no one can number
his sins.

X.

Maidens ! why should you worry in choosing whom
you shall marry ?
Choose whom you may, you will find you have
got somebody else.

XI.

Unto each man comes a day when his favourite
sins all forsake him,
And he complacently thinks he has forsaken his
sins.

XII.

Be not too anxious to gain your next-door neighbour's approval :
Live your own life, and let him strive your
approval to gain,

XIII.

Who would succeed in the world should be wise
    in the use of his pronouns.
Utter the You twenty times, where you once
    utter the I.

XIV.

The best-loved man or maid in the town would
    perish with anguish
Could they hear all that their friends say in the
    course of a day.

XV.

True luck consists not in holding the best of the
    cards at the table :
Luckiest he who knows just when to rise and
    go home.

XVI.

Pleasant enough it is to hear the world speak of
    your virtues ;
But in your secret heart 'tis of your faults you
    are proud.

XVII.

Try not to beat back the current, yet be not
    drowned in its waters ;
Speak with the speech of the world, think with
    the thoughts of the few.

XVIII.

Make all good men your well-wishers, and then,
    in the years' steady sifting,
Some of them turn into friends. Friends are
    the sunshine of life.

REGARDANT.

As I lay at your feet that afternoon,
Little we spoke,—you sat and mused,
Humming a sweet old-fashioned tune,

And I worshipped you, with a sense confused
Of the good time gone and the bad on the way,
While my hungry eyes your face perused

To catch and brand on my soul for aye
The subtle smile which had grown my doom.
Drinking sweet poison hushed I lay

Till the sunset shimmered athwart the room.
I rose to go.   You stood so fair
And dim in the dead day's tender gloom :

All at once, or ever I was aware,
Flashed from you on me a warm strong wave
Of passion and power ; in the silence there

I fell on my knees, like a lover, or slave,
With my wild hands clasping your slender
    waist ;
And my lips, with a sudden frenzy brave,

A madman's kiss on your girdle pressed,
And I felt your calm heart's quickening beat,
And your soft hands on me one instant rest.

And if God had loved me, how endlessly sweet
Had He let my heart in its rapture burst,
And throb its last at your firm small feet !

And when I was forth, I shuddered at first
At my imminent bliss.   As a soul in pain,
Treading his desolate path accursed,

Looks back and dreams through his tears'
      dim rain
That by Heaven's wide gate the angels smile,
Relenting, and beckon him back again,

And goes on, thrice damned by that devil's
      wile,—
So sometimes burns in my weary brain
The thought that you loved me all the while.

GUY OF THE TEMPLE.

DOWN the dim west slowly fails the stricken sun,
And from his hot face fades the crimson flush
Veiled in death's herald-shadows sick and grey.
Silent and dark the sombre valley lies
Forgotten ; happy in the late fond beams
Glimmer the constant waves of Galilee.
Afar, below, in airy music ring
The bugles of my host ; the column halts,
A wearied serpent glittering in the vale,
Where rising mist-like gleam the tented camps.

Pitch my pavilion here, where its high cross
May catch the last light lingering on the hill.
The savage shadows, struggling by the shore,
Have conquered in the valley ; inch by inch
The vanquished light fights bravely to these crags
To perish glorious in the sunset fire ;
Even as our hunted Cause so pressed and torn
In Syrian valleys, and the trampled marge
Of consecrated streams, displays at last
Its narrowing glories from these steadfast walls.
Here in God's name we stand, and brighter far
Shines the stern virtue of my martyr-host
Through these invidious fortunes, than of old,
When the still sunshine glinted on their helms,
And dallying breezes woke their bridle-bells
To tinkling music by the reedy shore
Of calm Tiberias, where our angry Lord,
Wroth at the deadly sin that cursed our camp,
Denied and blinded us, and gave us up
To the avenging sword of Saladin.
Yet would He not permit His truth to sink
To utter loss amid that foundering fight,

But led us, scarred and shattered from the spoil
Of Paynim rage, the desert's thirsty death,
To where beneath the sheltering crags we prayed
And rested and grew strong.   Heroes and saints
To alien peoples shall they be, my brave
And patient warriors ; for in their stout hearts
God's Spirit dwells for ever, and their hands
Are swift to do His service on His foes.
The swelling music of their vesper-hymn
Is rising fragrant from the shadowed vale
Familiar to the welcoming gates of heaven.

> *Mother of God ! as evening falls*
> *Upon the silent sea,*
> *And shadows veil the mountain walls,*
> *We lift our souls to thee !*
> *From lurking perils of the night,*
> *The desert's hidden harms,*
> *From plagues that waste, from blasts that*
> *smite,*
> *Defend thy men-at-arms !*

Ay ! Heaven keep them ! and ye angel-hosts
That wait with fluttering plumes around the great
White throne of God, guard them from scath
     and harm !
For in your starry records never shone
The memory of desert so great as theirs.
I hold not first, though peerless else on earth,
That knightly valour, born of gentle blood
And war's long tutelage, which hath made their
     name
Blaze like a baleful planet o'er these lands ;
Firm seat in saddle, lance unmoved, a hand
Wedding the hilt with death's persistent grasp ;
One-minded rush in fight that naught can stay.
Not these the highest, though I scorn not these,
But rather offer Heaven with humble heart
The deeds that Heaven hath given us arms to do.
For when God's smile was with us we were strong
To go like sudden lightning to our mark :

As on that summer day when Saladin—
Passing in scorn our host at Antioch,
Who spent the days in revel, and shamed the stars
With nightly scandal—came with all his host,
Its gay battalia brave with saffron silks,
Flaunting the banners of the Caliphate
Beneath the walls of fair Jerusalem :
And white and shaking came the Leper-King,
Great Baldwin's blasted scion, and Tripoli
And I, and twenty score of Temple Knights,
To meet the myriads marshalled by the bright
Untarnished flower of Eastern chivalry ;
A moment paused with level-fronting spears
And moveless helms before that shining host,
Whose gay attire abashed the morning light,
And then struck spur and charged, while from the
    mass
Of rushing terror burst the awful cry,
God and the Temple! As the avalanche slides
Down Alpine slopes, precipitous, cold and dark,
Unpitying and unwrathful, grinds and crushes
The mountain violets and the valley weeds,
And drags behind a trail of chaos and death ;
So burst we on that field, and through and
    through
The gay battalia brave with saffron silks,
Crushed and abolished every grace and gleam,
And dragged where'er we rode a sinuous track
Of chaos and death, till all the plain was filled
With battered armour, turbaned trunkless heads,
With silken mantles blushing angry gules
And Bagdad's banners trampled and forlorn.
And Saladin, stunned and bewildered sore,—
The greatest prince, save in the grace of God,
That now wears sword,—mounted his brother's
    barb,
And, followed by a half-score followers,
Sped to his castle Shaubec, over against
The cliffs by Ascalon, and there abode :
And sullenly made order that no more
The royal nouba should be played for him

Until he should erase the rusting stain
Upon his knightly honour ; and no more
The nouba sounded by the Sultan's tent,
Morning nor evening by the silent tent,
Until the headlong greed of Chatillon
Spread ruin on our cause from Montreale.
But greatest are my warriors, as I deem,
In that their hearts, nearer than any else,
Keep true the pledge of perfect purity
They pledged upon their sword-hilts long ago.
For all is possible to the pure in heart.

> *Mother of God ! thy starry smile*
> *Still bless us from above !*
> *Keep pure our souls from passion's guile,*
> *Our hearts from earthly love !*
> *Still save each soul from guilt apart*
> *As stainless as each sword,*
> *And guard undimmed in every heart*
> *The image of our Lord !*

O goodliest fellowship that the world has known,
True hearts and stalwart arms ! above your
    breasts
Glitters no flash of wreathen amulet
Forged against sword-stroke by the chanted
    rhythm
Of charms accurst ; but in each steadfast heart
Blazes the light of cloudless purity,
That like a splendid jewel glorifies
With restless fire the gold that spheres it round,
And marks you children of our God, whose lives
He guards with the awful jealousy of love.
And even me that generous love has spared,—
Me, trustless knight and miserable man,—
Sad prey of dark and mutinous thoughts that
    tempt
My sick soul into perjury and death—
Since His great love had pity on my pain,
Has spared to lead these blameless warriors safe
Into the desert from the blazing towns,

Out of the desert to the inviolate hills
Where God has roofed them with His hollow
    shield.
Through all these days of tempest and eclipse
His hand has led me and His wrath has flashed
Its lightnings in the pathway of my sword.
And so I hope, and so my crescent faith
Gains daily power, that all my prayers and tears
And toils and blood and anguish borne for Him
May blot the accusing of my deadly sin
From heaven's high compt, and give me rest in
    death ;
And lay the pallid ghost of mortal love,
That fills with banned and mournful loveliness,
Unblest, the haunted chambers of my soul.
My misery will atone,—my misery,—
Dear God, will surely atone ! for not the sting
Of lacerating thongs, nor the slow horror
Of crowns of thorny iron maddening the brows,
Nor all that else pale hermits have devised
To scourge the rebel senses in their shade
Of caverned desolation, have the power
To smart and goad and lash and mortify
Like the great love that binds my ruined heart
Relentless, as the insidious ivy binds
The shattered bulk of some deserted tower,
Enlacing slow and riving with strong hands
Of pitiless verdure every seam and jut,
Till none may tear it forth and save the tower.
So binds and masters me my hopeless love.
So through the desert, in the silent hills,
I' the current of the battle's storm and stress,
One thought has driven me,—that though men may
    call
Me stainless Paladin, Knight leal and true
To Christ and Our Lady, still I know myself
A knight not after God's own heart, a soul
Recreant, and whelmed in the forbidden sin.
For dearer to my sad heart than the cross
I give my heart's best blood for are the eyes
That long ago, when youth and hope were mine,

I loved in thy still valleys, far Provence!
And sweeter to my spirit than the bells
Of rescued Salem are the loving tones
Of her dear voice, soft echoing o'er the years.
They haunt me in the stillness and the glare
Of desert noontide when the horizon's line
Swims faintly throbbing, and my shadow hides
Skulking beneath me from the brassy sky.
And when night comes to soothe with breath of
    balm
And pomp of stars the worn and weary world,
Her eyes rise in my soul and make its day.
And even into the battle comes my love,   -
Snatching the duty that I offer Heaven.
   At closing of El-Majed's awful day,
When the last quivering sunbeams, choked with
    dust
And fume of blood, failed on the level plain,
In the last charge, when gathered all our knights
The precious handful who from morn had
    stemmed
The fury of the multitudinous hosts
Of Islam, where in youth's hot fire and pride
Ramped the young lion-whelp, Ben-Saladin ;
As down the slope we rode at eventide,
The dying sunlight faintly smiled to greet
Our tattered guidons and our dinted helms
And lance-heads blooming with the battle's rose.
Into the vale, dusk with the shadow of death,
With silent lips and ringing mail we rode.
And something in the spirit of the hour,
Or fate, or memory, or sorrow, or sin,
Or love, which unto me is all of these,
Possessed and bound me ; for when dashed our
    troop
In stormy clangour on the Paynim lines   -
The soul of my dead youth came into me ;
Faded away my oath ; the woes of Zion,
God was forgot ; blazed in my leaping heart,
With instant flash, life's inextinguished fires ;
Plunging along each tense limb poured the blood

Hot with its years of sleeping-smothered flame.
And in a dream I charged, and in a dream
I smote resistless ; foemen in my path
Fell unregarded, like the wayside flowers
Clipped by the truant's staff in daisied lanes.
For over me burned lustrous the dear eyes
Of my beloved ; I strove as at a joust
To gain at end the guerdon of her smile.
And ever, as in the dense mêlée I dashed,
Her name burst from my lips, as lightning breaks
Out of the plunging wrack of summer storms.

O my lost love ! Bright o'er the waste of years—
That bliss and beauty shines upon my soul ;
As far beyond yon desert hangs the sun,
Gilding with tender beam the barren stretch
Of sands that intervene. In this still light
The old sweet memories glimmer back to me,
Fair summers of my youth,—the idle days
I wandered in the bosky coverts hid
In the dim woods that girt my ancient home ;
The blue young eyes I met and worshipped there ;
The love that growing turned those gloomy wilds
To faery dells, and filled the vernal air
With light that bathed the hills of Paradise ;
The warm, long days of rapturous summer-time,
When through the forests thick and lush we
        strayed,
And love made our own sunshine in the shades.
And all things fair and graceful in the woods
I loved with liberal heart ; the violets
Were dear for her dear eyes, the quiring birds
That caught the musical tremble of her voice.
O happy twilights in the leafy glooms !
When in the glowing dusk the winsome arts
And maiden graces that all day had kept
Us twain and separate melted away
In blushing silence, and my love was mine
Utterly, utterly, with clinging arms
And quick, caressing fingers, warm red lips,
Where vows, half uttered, drowned in kisses, died ;

Mine, with the starlight in her passionate eyes ;
The wild wind of the woodland breathing low
To wake the elfin music of the leaves,
And free the prisoned odours of the flowers,
In honour of young Love come to his throne !
While we under the stars, with twining arms
And mutual lips insatiate, gave our souls—
Madly forgetting earth and heaven—to love !

> *In desert march or battle flame,*
>   *In fortress and in field,*
> *Our war-cry is thy holy name,*
>   *Thy love our joy and shield !*
> *And if we falter, let thy power*
>   *Thy stern avenger be,*
> *And God forget us in the hour*
>   *We cease to think of thee !*

Curse me not, God of Justice and of Love !
Pitiful God, let my long woe atone !

I cannot deem but God has pitied me ;
Else why with painful care have I been saved,
Whenever tossed and drenched in the fierce tide
Of Saladin's victories by the walls profaned
Of Jaffa, on the sands of far Daroum,
Or in the battle thundering on the downs
Of Ramlah, or the bloody day that shed
Red horrors on high Gaza's parapets ?
For never a storm of fatal fight has raged
In Islam's track of rout and ruin swept
From Egypt to Gebail, but when the ebb
Of battle came I and my host have lain,
Scarred, scorched, safe somewhere on its fiery
    shore.
At Marcab's lingering siege, where day by day
We told the Moslem legions toiling slow,
Planting their engines, delving in their mines
To quench in our destruction this last light
Of Christendom, our fortress in the crags,

God's beacon swung defiant from the stars ;
One thunderous night I knew their miners groped
Below, and thought ere morn to die, in crush
And tumult of the falling citadel.
And pondering of my fate—the broken storm
Sobbing its life away—I was aware
There grew between me and the quieting skies
A face and form I knew,—not as in dreams,
The sad dishevelled loveliness of earth,
But lighter than the thin air where she swayed,—
Gold hair flame-fluttered, eyes and mouth aglow
With lambent light of spiritual joy.
With sweet command she beckoned me away
And led me vaguely dreaming, till I saw
Where the wild flood in sudden fury had burst
A passage through the rocks : and thence I led
My host unharmed, following her luminous eyes,
Until the east was grey, and with a smile
Wooing me heavenward still she passed away
Into the rosy trouble of the dawn.

And I believe my love is shrived in heaven,
And I believe that I shall soon be free.

For ever, as I journey on, to me
Waking or sleeping come faint whisperings
And fancies not of earth, as if the gates
Of near eternity stood for me ajar,
And ghostly gales come blowing o'er my soul
Fraught with the amaranth odours of the skies.
I go to join the Lion-Heart at Acre,
And there, after due homage to my liege,
And after patient penance of the Church,
And after final devoir in the fight,
If that my God be gracious, I shall die.
And so I pray—Lord, pardon if I sin !—
That I may lose in death's embittered wave
The stain of sinful loving, and may find
In glory again the love I lost below,
With all of fair and bright and unattained,

Beautiful in the cherishing smile of God,
By the glad waters of the River of Life!

Night hangs above the valley; dies the day
In peace, casting his last glance on my cross,
And warns me to my prayers. *Ave Maria!*

> *Mother of God! the evening fades*
>   *On wave and hill and lea,*
> *And in the twilight's deepening shades*
>   *We lift our souls to thee!*
> *In passion's stress—the battle's strife,*
>   *The desert's lurking harms,*
> *Maid-Mother of the Lord of Life*
>   *Protect thy men-at-arms!*

Translations.

—✦—

THE WAY TO HEAVEN.

FROM THE GERMAN.

ONE day the Sultan, grand and grim,
Ordered the Mufti brought to him.
" Now let thy wisdom solve for me
The question I shall put to thee.

" The different tribes beneath my sway
Four several sects of priests obey ;
Now tell me which of all the four
Is on the path to Heaven's door."

The Sultan spake, and then was dumb.
The Mufti looked about the room,
And straight made answer to his lord,
Fearing the bowstring at each word :

" Thou, godlike in thy lofty birth,
Who art our Allah upon earth,
Illume me with thy favouring ray,
And I will answer as I may.

" Here, where thou thronest in thy hall,
I see there are four doors in all ;
And through all four thy slaves may gaze
Upon the brightness of thy face.

" That I came hither safely through
Was to thy gracious message due,
And, blinded by thy splendour's flame,
I cannot tell the way I came."

COUNTESS JUTTA.

FROM THE GERMAN OF HEINRICH HEINE.

THE Countess Jutta passed over the Rhine
In a light canoe by the moon's pale shine.
The handmaid rows and the Countess speaks:
" Seest thou not there where the water breaks
          Seven corpses swim
          In the moonlight dim?
So sorrowful swim the dead !

" They were seven knights full of fire and youth,
They sank on my heart and swore me truth.
I trusted them ; but for Truth's sweet sake,
Lest they should be tempted their oaths to break,
          I had them bound,
          And tenderly drowned !
So sorrowful swim the dead ! "

The merry Countess laughed outright !
It rang so wild in the startled night !
Up to the waist the dead men rise
And stretch lean fingers to the skies.
          They nod and stare
          With a glassy glare !
So sorrowful swim the dead !

A BLESSING.

AFTER HEINE.

WHEN I look on thee and feel how dear,
How pure, and how fair thou art,
Into my eyes there steals a tear,
And a shadow mingled of love and fear
Creeps slowly over my heart.

And my very hands feel as if they would lay
Themselves on thy fair young head,
And pray the good God to keep thee alway
As good and lovely, as pure and gay,—
When I and my wild love are dead.

TO THE YOUNG.

AFTER HEINE.

LET your feet not falter, your course not alter
  By golden apples, till victory's won !
The sword's sharp clangour, the dart's shrill anger,
  Swerve not the hero thundering on.

A bold beginning is half the winning,
  An Alexander makes worlds his fee.
No long debating !   The Queens are waiting
  In his pavilion on bended knee.

Thus swift pursuing his wars and wooing,
  He mounts old Darius' bed and throne.
O glorious ruin !   O blithe undoing !
  O drunk death-triumph in Babylon !

THE GOLDEN CALF.

AFTER HEINE.

DOUBLE flutes and horns resound
As they dance the idol round ;
Jacob's daughters, madly reeling,
  Whirl about the golden calf.
      Hear them laugh !
Kettledrums and laughter pealing.

Dresses tucked above their knees,
Maids of noblest families,
In the swift dance blindly wheeling,
  Circle in their wild career
      Round the steer,—
Kettledrums and laughter pealing.

Aaron's self, the guardian grey
Of the faith, at last gives way,
Madness all his senses stealing ;
  Prances in his high priest's coat
      Like a goat,—
Kettledrums and laughter pealing.

THE AZRA.

AFTER HEINE.

DAILY walked the fair and lovely
Sultan's daughter in the twilight,—
In the twilight by the fountain,
Where the sparkling waters plash.

Daily stood the young slave silent
In the twilight by the fountain,
Where the plashing waters sparkle,
Pale and paler every day.

Once by twilight came the princess
Up to him with rapid questions :
" I would know thy name, thy nation,
Whence thou comest, who thou art."

And the young slave said, " My name is
Mahomet, I come from Yemmen.
I am of the sons of Azra,
Men who perish if they love."

GOOD AND BAD LUCK.

AFTER HEINE.

GOOD luck is the gayest of all gay girls,
   Long in one place she will not stay;
Back from your brow she strokes the curls,
   Kisses you quick and flies away.

But Madame Bad Luck soberly comes
   And stays,—no fancy has she for flitting,—
Snatches of true love-songs she hums,
   And sits by your bed, and brings her knitting.

L'AMOUR DU MENSONGE.

AFTER CHARLES BAUDELAIRE.

WHEN I behold thee, O my indolent love,
  To the sound of ringing brazen melodies,
Through garish halls harmoniously move,
  Scattering a scornful light from languid eyes;

When I see, smitten by the blazing lights,
  Thy pale front, beauteous in its bloodless glow
As the faint fires that deck the Northern nights,
  And eyes that draw me wheresoe'er I go;

I say, She is fair, too coldly strange for speech;
  A crown of memories, her calm brow above,
Shines; and her heart is like a bruised red peach,
  Ripe as her body for intelligent love.

Art thou late fruit of spicy savour and scent?
  A funeral vase awaiting tearful showers?
An Eastern odour, waste and oasis blent?
  A silken cushion or a bank of flowers?

I know there are eyes of melancholy sheen
  To which no passionate secrets e'er were given;
Shrines where no god or saint has ever been,
  As deep and empty as the vault of Heaven.

But what care I if this be all pretence?
  'Twill serve a heart that seeks for truth no more.
All one thy folly or indifference,—
  Hail, lovely mask, thy beauty I adore!

AMOR MYSTICUS.

FROM THE SPANISH OF SOR MARCELA DE CARPIO.

Let them say to my Lover
    That here I lie!
The thing of His pleasure,
    His slave am I.

Say that I seek Him
    Only for love,
And welcome are tortures
    My passion to prove.

Love giving gifts
    Is suspicious and cold;
I have all, my Belovèd,
    When Thee I hold.

Hope and devotion
    The good may gain;
I am but worthy
    Of passion and pain.

So noble a Lord
    None serves in vain,
For the pay of my love
    Is my love's sweet pain.

I love Thee, to love Thee,—
    No more I desire;
By faith is nourished
    My love's strong fire.

I kiss Thy hands
    When I feel their blows ;
In the place of caresses
    Thou givest me woes.

But in Thy chastising
    Is joy and peace.
O Master and Love,
    Let Thy blows not cease.

Thy beauty, Belovèd,
    With scorn is rife,
But I know that Thou lovest me,
    Better than life.

And because thou lovest me,
    Lover of mine,
Death can but make me
    Utterly Thine.

I die with longing
    Thy face to see ;
Oh ! sweet is the anguish
    Of death to me !

THE

VISION OF DON RODERICK,

AND

THE FIELD OF WATERLOO.

BY

WALTER SCOTT.

———

" Quid dignum memorare tuis, Hispania, terris,
Vox humana valet ! "—CLAUDIAN.

PREFACE

TO THE VISION OF DON RODERICK.

—◦◦◦—

THE following Poem is founded upon a Spanish
Tradition, bearing, in general, that Don Roderick,
the last Gothic King of Spain, when the invasion
of the Moors was depending, had the temerity
to descend into an ancient vault, near Toledo, the
opening of which had been denounced as fatal to
the Spanish Monarchy. The legend adds, that
his rash curiosity was mortified by an emblematical
representation of those Saracens who, in the year
714, defeated him in battle, and reduced Spain
under their dominion. I have presumed to pro-
long the Vision of the Revolutions of Spain down
to the present eventful crisis of the Peninsula, and
to divide it, by a supposed change of scene, into
THREE PERIODS. The FIRST of these represents
the Invasion of the Moors, the Defeat and Death
of Roderick, and closes with the peaceful occupa-
tion of the country by the victors. The SECOND
PERIOD embraces the state of the Peninsula when
the conquests of the Spaniards and Portuguese in
the East and West Indies had raised to the highest
pitch the renown of their arms; sullied, however,
by superstition and cruelty. An allusion to the

inhumanities of the Inquisition terminates this picture. The LAST PART of the Poem opens with the state of Spain previous to the unparalleled treachery of BUONAPARTE, gives a sketch of the usurpation attempted upon that unsuspicious and friendly kingdom, and terminates with the arrival of the British succours. It may be further proper to mention, that the object of the Poem is less to commemorate or detail particular incidents, than to exhibit a general and impressive picture of the several periods brought upon the stage.

EDINBURGH, *June* 24, 1811.

The Vision of Don Roderick.

—◦⊱⊰◦—

INTRODUCTION.

I

LIVES there a strain, whose sounds of mounting
    fire
    May rise distinguished o'er the din of war ;
Or died it with yon Master of the Lyre
    Who sung beleaguered Ilion's evil star ?
Such, WELLINGTON, might reach thee from afar,
    Wafting its descant wide o'er Ocean's range ;
Nor shouts, nor clashing arms, its mood could
    mar,
    All, as it swelled 'twixt each loud trumpet-
    change,
That clangs to Britain victory, to Portugal revenge !

II.

Yes ! such a strain, with all o'er-pouring measure,
    Might melodise with each tumultuous sound
Each voice of fear or triumph, woe or pleasure,
    That rings Mondego's ravaged shores around ;
The thundering cry of hosts with conquest
    crowned,
    The female shriek, the ruined peasant's moan,
The shout of captives from their chains unbound,
    The foiled oppressor's deep and sullen groan,
A Nation's choral hymn, for tyranny o'erthrown.

III.

But we, weak minstrels of a laggard day
  Skilled but to imitate an elder page,
Timid and raptureless, can we repay
  The debt thou claim'st in this exhausted age?
Thou givest our lyres a theme, that might en-
    gage
  Those that could send thy name o'er sea and
    land,
While sea and land shall last; for Homer's rage
  A theme; a theme for Milton's mighty hand—
How much unmeet for us, a faint degenerate band!

IV.

Ye mountains stern! within whose rugged breast
  The friends of Scottish freedom found repose;
Ye torrents! whose hoarse sounds have soothed
    their rest,
  Returning from the field of vanquished foes;
Say, have ye lost each wild majestic close
  That erst the choir of Bards or Druids flung,
What time their hymn of victory arose,
  And Cattraeth's glens with voice of triumph
    rung,
And mystic Merlin harped, and grey-haired
    Llywarch sung?

V.

Oh! if your wilds such minstrelsy retain,
  As sure your changeful gales seem oft to say,
When sweeping wild and sinking soft again,
  Like trumpet-jubilee, or harp's wild sway;
If ye can echo such triumphant lay,
  Then lend the note to him has loved you long!
Who pious gathered each tradition grey
  That floats your solitary wastes along,
And with affection vain gave them new voice in
    song.

VI.

For not till now, how oft soe'er the task
  Of truant verse hath lightened graver care,
From Muse or Sylvan was he wont to ask,
  In phrase poetic, inspiration fair;
Careless he gave his numbers to the air,
  They came unsought for, if applauses came:
Nor for himself prefers he now the prayer;
  Let but his verse befit a hero's fame,
Immortal be the verse!—forgot the poet's name!

VII.

Hark, from yon misty cairn their answer tost:
  "Minstrel! the fame of whose romantic lyre,
Capricious-swelling now, may soon be lost,
  Like the light flickering of a cottage fire;
If to such task presumptuous thou aspire,
  Seek not from us the meed to warrior due:
Age after age has gathered son to sire
  Since our grey cliffs the din of conflict knew,
Or, pealing through our vales, victorious bugles
    blew.

VIII.

"Decayed our old traditionary lore,
  Save where the lingering fays renew their
    ring,
By milkmaid seen beneath the hawthorn hoar,
  Or round the marge of Minchmore's haunted
    spring;
Save where their legends grey-haired shepherds
    sing,
  That now scarce win a listening ear but
    thine,
Of feuds obscure, and Border ravaging,
  And rugged deeds recount in rugged line,
Of moonlight foray made on Teviot, Tweed, or
    Tyne.

IX.

"No! search romantic lands, where the near
  Sun
 Gives with unstinted boon ethereal flame,
Where the rude villager, his labour done,
 In verse spontaneous chants some favoured
  name,
Whether Olalia's charms his tribute claim,
 Her eye of diamond, and her locks of jet ;
Or whether, kindling at the deeds of Græme,
 He sing, to wild Morisco measure set,
Old Albin's red claymore, green Erin's bayonet !

X.

"Explore those regions, where the flinty crest
 Of wild Nevada ever gleams with snows,
Where in the proud Alhambra's ruined breast
 Barbaric monuments of pomp repose ;
Or where the banners of more ruthless foes
 Than the fierce Moor, float o'er Toledo's
  fane,
From whose tall towers even now the patriot
  throws
 An anxious glance, to spy upon the plain
The blended ranks of England, Portugal, and
  Spain.

XI.

"There, of Numantian fire a swarthy spark
 Still lightens in the sunburnt native's eye ;
The stately port, slow step, and visage dark,
 Still mark enduring pride and constancy.
And, if the glow of feudal chivalry
 Beam not, as once, thy nobles' dearest pride,
Iberia ! oft thy crestless peasantry
 Have seen the plumed Hidalgo quit their side,
Have seen, yet dauntless stood—'gainst fortune
  fought and died.

XII.

"And cherished still by that unchanging race,
   Are themes for minstrelsy more high than
      thine ;
Of strange tradition many a mystic trace,
   Legend and vision, prophecy and sign ;
Where wonders wild of Arabesque combine
   With Gothic imagery of darker shade,
Forming a model meet for minstrel line.
   Go, seek such theme !"—the Mountain Spirit
      said.
With filial awe I heard—I heard, and I obeyed.

The Vision of Don Roderick.

—⁂—

I.

REARING their crests amid the cloudless skies,
 And darkly clustering in the pale moonlight,
Toledo's holy towers and spires arise,
 As from a trembling lake of silver white.
Their mingled shadows intercept the sight
 Of the broad burial-ground outstretched below,
And nought disturbs the silence of the night ;
 All sleeps in sullen shade, or silver glow,
All save the heavy swell of Teio's ceaseless flow.

II.

All save the rushing swell of Teio's tide,
 Or, distant heard, a courser's neigh or tramp ;
Their changing rounds as watchful horsemen ride,
 To guard the limits of King Roderick's camp.
For through the river's night-fog rolling damp
 Was many a proud pavilion dimly seen,
Which glimmered back, against the moon's fair
  lamp,
Tissues of silk and silver twisted sheen,
And standards proudly pitched, and warders armed
  between.

III.

But of their Monarch's person keeping ward,
 Since last the deep-mouthed bell of vespers
  tolled,
The chosen soldiers of the royal guard
 The post beneath the proud Cathedral hold :

140

A band unlike their Gothic sires of old,
　Who, for the cap of steel and iron mace,
Bear slender darts, and casques bedecked with
　　gold,
　While silver-studded belts their shoulders grace,
Where ivory quivers ring in the broad falchion's
　　place.

IV.

In the light language of an idle court,
　They murmured at their master's long delay,
And held his lengthened orisons in sport :—
　"What! will Don Roderick here till morning
　　　stay,
To wear in shrift and prayer the night away?
　And are his hours in such dull penance past,
For fair Florinda's plundered charms to pay?"
　Then to the east their weary eyes they cast,
And wished the lingering dawn would glimmer forth
　　at last.

V.

But, far within, Toledo's Prelate lent
　An ear of fearful wonder to the King ;
The silver lamp a fitful lustre sent,
　So long that sad confession witnessing :
For Roderick told of many a hidden thing,
　Such as are lothly uttered to the air,
When Fear, Remorse, and Shame the bosom
　　wring,
　And Guilt his secret burden cannot bear,
And Conscience seeks in speech a respite from
　　Despair.

VI.

Full on the Prelate's face, and silver hair,
　The stream of failing light was feebly rolled :
But Roderick's visage, though his head was bare,
　Was shadowed by his hand and mantle's fold.

While of his hidden soul the sins he told,
　Proud Alaric's descendant could not brook,
That mortal man his bearing should behold,
　Or boast that he had seen, when Conscience
　　shook,
Fear tame a monarch's brow, Remorse a warrior's
　look.

VII.

The old man's faded cheek waxed yet more pale,
　As many a secret sad the King bewrayed ;
As sign and glance eked out the unfinished tale,
　When in the midst his faltering whisper stayed.
" Thus royal Witiza was slain,"—he said ;
　" Yet, holy Father, deem not it was I."
Thus still Ambition strives her crimes to shade.—
　" Oh, rather deem 'twas stern necessity !
Self-preservation bade, and I must kill or die.

VIII.

" And if Florinda's shrieks alarmed the air,
　If she invoked her absent sire in vain,
And on her knees implored that I would spare,
　Yet, reverend Priest, thy sentence rash refrain !
All is not as it seems—the female train
　Know by their bearing to disguise their
　　mood : "
But Conscience here, as if in high disdain,
　Sent to the Monarch's cheek the burning
　　blood—
He stayed his speech abrupt—and up the Prelate
　stood.

IX.

" O hardened offspring of an iron race !
　What of thy crimes, Don Roderick, shall I say?
What alms, or prayers, or penance can efface
　Murder's dark spot, wash treason's stain away !

For the foul ravisher how shall I pray,
  Who, scarce repentant, makes his crime his
    boast?
How hope Almighty vengeance shall delay,
  Unless, in mercy to yon Christian host,
He spare the shepherd, lest the guiltless sheep
  be lost?"

X.

Then kindled the dark tyrant in his mood,
  And to his brow returned its dauntless gloom ;
" And welcome then," he cried, " be blood for
    blood,
For treason treachery, for dishonour doom !
Yet will I know whence come they, or by whom.
  Show, for thou canst—give forth the fated key,
And guide me, Priest, to that mysterious room,
  Where, if aught true in old tradition be,
His nation's future fates a Spanish King shall
  see."

XI.

" Ill-fated Prince ! recall the desperate word,
  Or pause ere yet the omen thou obey !
Bethink, yon spell-bound portal would afford
  Never to former Monarch entrance-way ;
Nor shall it ever ope, old records say,
  Save to a King, the last of all his line,
What time his empire totters to decay,
  And treason digs, beneath, her fatal mine,
And, high above, impends avenging wrath divine."—

XII.

" Prelate ! a Monarch's fate brooks no delay ;
  Lead on !"—The ponderous key the old man
    took,
And held the winking lamp, and led the way,
  By winding stair, dark aisle, and secret nook,

Then on an ancient gateway bent his look ;
  And, as the key the desperate King essayed,
Low muttered thunders the Cathedral shook,
  And twice he stopped, and twice new effort
    made,
Till the huge bolts rolled back, and the loud hinges
    brayed.

XIII.

Long, large, and lofty was that vaulted hall ;
  Roof, walls, and floor were all of marble stone,
Of polished marble, black as funeral pall,
  Carved o'er with signs and characters unknown.
A paly light, as of the dawning, shone
  Through the sad bounds, but whence they
    could not spy ;
For window to the upper air was none ;
  Yet, by that light, Don Roderick could descry
Wonders that ne'er till then were seen by mortal eye.

XIV.

Grim sentinels, against the upper wall,
  Of molten bronze, two Statues held their place ;
Massive their naked limbs, their stature tall,
  Their frowning foreheads golden circles grace.
Moulded they seemed for kings of giant race,
  That lived and sinned before the avenging
    flood ;
This grasped a scythe, that rested on a mace ;
  This spread his wings for flight, that pondering
    stood,
Each stubborn seemed and stern, immutable of
    mood.

XV.

Fixed was the right-hand Giant's brazen look
  Upon his brother's glass of shifting sand,
As if its ebb he measured by a book,
  Whose iron volume loaded his huge hand ;

In which was wrote of many a fallen land
Of empires lost, and kings to exile driven :
And o'er that pair their names in scroll expand—
  " Lo, DESTINY and TIME ! to whom by
    Heaven
The guidance of the earth is for a season given."—

XVI.

Even while they read, the sand-glass wastes
    away ;
And, as the last and lagging grains did creep,
That right-hand Giant 'gan his club upsway,
  As one that startles from a heavy sleep.
Full on the upper wall the mace's sweep
  At once descended with the force of thunder,
And hurtling down at once, in crumbled heap,
  The marble boundary was rent asunder,
And gave to Roderick's view new sights of fear
    and wonder.

XVII.

For they might spy, beyond that mighty breach,
  Realms as of Spain in visioned prospect laid,
Castles and towers, in due proportion each,
  As by some skilful artist's hand portrayed :
Here, crossed by many a wild Sierra's shade,
  And boundless plains that tire the traveller's
    eye ;
There, rich with vineyard and with olive glade,
  Or deep-embrowned by forests huge and high,
Or washed by mighty streams, that slowly mur-
    mured by.

XVIII.

And here, as erst upon the antique stage
  Passed forth the band of masquers trimly led,
In various forms, and various equipage,
  While fitting strains the hearer's fancy fed ;

G

So, to sad Roderick's eye in order spread,
　Successive pageants filled that mystic scene,
Showing the fate of battles ere they bled,
　And issue of events that had not been ;
And, ever and anon, strange sounds were heard
　　between.

XIX.

First shrilled an unrepeated female shriek !—
　It seemed as if Don Roderick knew the call,
For the bold blood was blanching in his cheek.—
　Then answered kettle-drum and attabal,
Gong-peal and cymbal-clank the ear appal,
　The Tecbir war-cry, and the Lelie's yell,
Ring wildly dissonant along the hall.
　Needs not to Roderick their dread import
　　tell—
" The Moor !" he cried, "the Moor !—ring out
　the Tocsin bell !

XX.

" They come ! they come ! I see the groaning
　　lands
　White with the turbans of each Arab horde ;
Swart Zaarah joins her misbelieving bands,
　Alla and Mahomet their battle-word,
The choice they yield, the Koran or the Sword—
　See how the Christians rush to arms amain !—
In yonder shout the voice of conflict roared,
　The shadowy hosts are closing on the plain—
Now, God and Saint Iago strike, for the good cause
　of Spain !

XXI.

" By Heaven, the Moors prevail ! the Christians
　　yield !
　Their coward leader gives for flight the sign !
The sceptred craven mounts to quit the field—
　Is not yon steed Orelio ?—Yes, 'tis mine !

But never was she turned from battle-line :
   Lo ! where the recreant spurs o'er stock and
      stone !—
Curses pursue the slave, and wrath divine !
   Rivers ingulph him !"—" Hush," in shudder-
      ing tone,
The Prelate said; "rash Prince, yon visioned
      form's thine own."

XXII.

Just then, a torrent crossed the flier's course ;
   The dangerous ford the Kingly Likeness tried ;
But the deep eddies whelmed both man and horse,
   Swept like benighted peasant down the tide ;
And the proud Moslemah spread far and wide,
   As numerous as their native locust band ;
Berber and Ismael's sons the spoils divide,
   With naked scimitars mete out the land,
And for the bondsmen base the free-born natives
      brand.

XXIII.

Then rose the grated Harem, to enclose
   The loveliest maidens of the. Christian line ;
Then, menials, to their misbelieving foes,
   Castile's young nobles held forbidden wine ;
Then, too, the holy Cross, salvation's sign,
   By impious hands was from the altar thrown,
And the deep aisles of the polluted shrine
   Echoed, for holy hymn and organ-tone,
The Santon's frantic dance, the Fakir's gibbering
      moan.

XXIV.

How fares Don Roderick?—E'en as one who spies
   Flames dart their glare o'er midnight's sable
      woof,
And hears around his children's piercing cries,
   And sees the pale assistants stand aloof;

While cruel Conscience brings him bitter proof,
  His folly, or his crime, have caused his grief;
And while above him nods the crumbling roof,
  He curses earth and Heaven — himself in
    chief—
Desperate of earthly aid, despairing Heaven's relief!

XXV.

That scythe-armed Giant turned his fatal glass
  And twilight on the landscape closed her wings;
Far to Asturian hills the war-sounds pass,
  And in their stead rebeck or timbrel rings;
And to the sound the bell-decked dancer springs,
  Bazars resound as when their marts are met,
In tourney light the Moor his jerrid flings,
  And on the land as evening seemed to set,
The Imaum's chant was heard from mosque or
    minaret.

XXVI.

So passed that pageant. Ere another came,
  The visionary scene was wrapped in smoke
Whose sulph'rous wreaths were crossed by sheets
    of flame;
  With every flash a bolt explosive broke,
Till Roderick deemed the fiends had burst their
    yoke,
  And waved 'gainst heaven the infernal gon-
    falone!
For War a new and dreadful language spoke,
  Never by ancient warrior heard or known;
Lightning and smoke her breath, and thunder was
    her tone.

XXVII.

From the dim landscape rolled the clouds away—
  The Christians have regained their heritage;
Before the Cross has waned the Crescent's ray,
  And many a monastery decks the stage,

And lofty church, and low-browed hermitage.
The land obeys a Hermit and a Knight,—
The Genii those of Spain for many an age;
This clad in sackcloth, that in armour bright,
And that was VALOUR named, this BIGOTRY was
    hight.

XXVIII.

VALOUR was harnessed like a chief of old,
    Armed at all points, and prompt for knightly
        gest;
His sword was tempered in the Ebro cold,
    Morena's eagle plume adorned his crest,
The spoils of Afric's lion bound his breast.
    Fierce he stepped forward and flung down his
        gage;
As if of mortal kind to brave the best.
    Him followed his Companion, dark and sage,
As he, my Master, sung the dangerous Archimage.

XXIX.

Haughty of heart and brow the Warrior came,
    In look and language proud as proud might be,
Vaunting his lordship, lineage, fights, and fame:
    Yet was that barefoot Monk more proud
        than he:
And as the ivy climbs the tallest tree,
    So round the loftiest soul his toils he wound,
And with his spells subdued the fierce and free,
    Till ermined Age and Youth in arms renowned,
Honouring his scourge and haircloth, meekly kissed
        the ground.

XXX.

And thus it chanced that VALOUR, peerless
        knight,
    Who ne'er to King or Kaiser vailed his crest,
Victorious still in bull-feast or in fight,
    Since first his limbs with mail he did invest,

Stooped ever to that Anchoret's behest ;
  Nor reasoned of the right, nor of the wrong,
But at his bidding laid the lance in rest,
  And wrought fell deeds the troubled world
    along,
For he was fierce as brave, and pitiless as strong.

XXXI.

Oft his proud galleys sought some new-found
    world,
  That latest sees the sun, or first the morn ;
Still at that Wizard's feet their spoils he hurled,—
  Ingots of ore from rich Potosi borne,
Crowns by Caciques, aigrettes by Omrahs worn,
  Wrought of rare gems, but broken, rent, and
    foul ;
Idols of gold from heathen temples torn,
  Bedabbled all with blood.—With grisly scowl
The Hermit marked the stains, and smiled beneath
    his cowl.

XXXII.

Then did he bless the offering, and bade make
  Tribute to Heaven of gratitude and praise ;
And at his word the choral hymns awake,
  And many a hand the silver censer sways,
But with the incense-breath these censers raise,
  Mix steams from corpses smouldering in the
    fire ;
The groans of prisoned victims mar the lays,
  And shrieks of agony confound the quire ;
While, 'mid the mingled sounds, the darkened
    scenes expire.

XXXIII.

Preluding light, were strains of music heard,
  As once again revolved that measured sand ;
Such sounds as when, for silvan dance prepared,
  Gay Xeres summons forth her vintage band ;

When for the light bolero ready stand
    The mozo blithe, with gay muchacha met,
He conscious of his broidered cap and band,
    She of her netted locks and light corsette,
Each tiptoe perched to spring, and shake the
        castanet.

XXXIV.

And well such strains the opening scene became ;
    For VALOUR had relaxed his ardent look,
And at a lady's feet, like lion tame,
    Lay stretched, full loath the weight of arms to
        brook ;
And softened BIGOTRY, upon his book,
    Pattered a task of little good or ill :
But the blithe peasant plied his pruning-hook,
    Whistled the muleteer o'er vale and hill,
And rung from village-green the merry seguidille.

XXXV.

Grey Royalty, grown impotent of toil,
    Let the grave sceptre slip his lazy hold ;
And, careless, saw his rule become the spoil
    Of a loose Female and her minion bold.
But peace was on the cottage and the fold,
    From Court intrigue, from bickering faction
        far ;
Beneath the chestnut-tree Love's tale was told,
    And to the tinkling of the light guitar,
Sweet stooped the western sun, sweet rose the
        evening star.

XXXVI.

As that sea-cloud, in size like human hand,
    When first from Carmel by the Tishbite seen,
Came slowly overshadowing Israel's land,
    A while, perchance, bedecked with colours
        sheen,

While yet the sunbeams on its skirts had been,
  Limning with purple and with gold its shroud,
Till darker folds obscured the blue serene
  And blotted heaven with one broad sable
    cloud,
Then sheeted rain burst down, and whirlwinds
    howled aloud :—

XXXVII.

Even so, upon that peaceful scene was poured,
  Like gathering clouds, full many a foreign
    band,
And HE, their Leader, wore in sheath his sword,
  And offered peaceful front and open hand,
Veiling the perjured treachery he planned,
  By friendship's zeal and honour's specious guise,
Until he won the passes of the land ;
  Then burst were honour's oath and friend-
    ship's ties !
He clutched his vulture grasp, and called fair Spain
    his prize.

XXXVIII.

An iron crown his anxious forehead bore ;
  And well such diadem his heart became,
Who ne'er his purpose for remorse gave o'er,
  Or checked his course for piety or shame ;
Who, trained a soldier, deemed a soldier's fame
  Might flourish in the wreath of battles won,
Though neither truth nor honour decked his
    name ;
  Who, placed by fortune on a Monarch's throne,
Recked not of Monarch's faith, or Mercy's kingly
    tone.

XXXIX.

From a rude isle his ruder lineage came,
  The spark, that, from a suburb-hovel's hearth
Ascending, wraps some capital in flame,
  Hath not a meaner or more sordid birth.

And for the soul that bade him waste the earth—
  The sable land-flood from some swamp ob-
    scure
That poisons the glad husband - field with
    dearth,
  And by destruction bids its fame endure,
Hath not a source more sullen, stagnant, and
    impure.

XL.

Before that Leader strode a shadowy Form ;
  Her limbs like mist, her torch like meteor
    showed,
With which she beckoned him through fight and
    storm,
  And all he crushed that crossed his desperate
    road,
Nor thought, nor feared, nor looked on what he
    trode.
  Realms could not glut his pride, blood could
    not slake,
So oft as e'er she shook her torch abroad—
  It was AMBITION bade her terrors wake,
Nor deigned she, as of yore, a milder form to
    take.

XLI.

No longer now she spurned at mean revenge,
  Or stayed her hand for conquered foeman's
    moan ;
As when, the fates of aged Rome to change,
  By Cæsar's side she crossed the Rubicon.
Nor joyed she to bestow the spoils she won,
  As when the banded powers of Greece were
    tasked
To war beneath the Youth of Macedon :
  No seemly veil her modern minion asked,
He saw her hideous face, and loved the fiend un-
    masked.

XLII.

That Prelate marked his march — On banners
    blazed
  With battles won in many a distant land,
On eagle-standards and on arms he gazed;
    "And hopest thou, then," he said, "thy power
    shall stand?
Oh! thou hast builded on the shifting sand,
    And thou hast tempered it with slaughter's
    flood;
And know, fell scourge in the Almighty's hand,
    Gore-moistened trees shall perish in the bud,
And by a bloody death shall die the Man of
    Blood!"

XLIII.

The ruthless Leader beckoned from his train
  A wan fraternal Shade, and bade him kneel,
And paled his temples with the crown of Spain,
    While trumpets rang, and heralds cried "Cas-
    tile!"
Not that he loved him—No!—In no man's weal,
  Scarce in his own, e'er joyed that sullen heart;
Yet round that throne he bade his warriors
    wheel,
    That the poor puppet might perform his part,
And be a sceptred slave, at his stern beck to start.

XLIV.

But on the Natives of that Land misused,
  Not long the silence of amazement hung,
Nor brooked they long their friendly faith abused;
    For, with a common shriek, the general tongue
Exclaimed, "To arms!"—and fast to arms they
    sprung.
And VALOUR woke, that Genius of the Land!
Pleasure, and ease, and sloth aside he flung,
  As burst the awakening Nazarite his band,
When 'gainst his treacherous foes he clenched his
    dreadful hand.

XLV.

That Mimic Monarch now cast anxious eye
    Upon the Satraps that begirt him round,
Now doffed his royal robe in act to fly,
    And from his brow the diadem unbound.
So oft, so near, the Patriot bugle wound,
    From Tarik's walls to Bilboa's mountains
      blown,
These martial satellites hard labour found
    To guard awhile his substituted throne—
Light recking of his cause, but battling for their
    own.

XLVI.

From Alpuhara's peak that bugle rung,
    And it was echoed from Corunna's wall ;
Stately Seville responsive war-shot flung,
    Grenada caught it in her Moorish hall ;
Galicia bade her children fight or fall,
    Wild Biscay shook his mountain-coronet,
Valencia roused her at the battle-call,
    And, foremost still where Valour's sons are
      met,
First started to his gun each fiery Miquelet.

XLVII.

But unappalled, and burning for the fight,
    The Invaders march, of victory secure ;
Skilful their force to sever or unite,
    And trained alike to vanquish or endure.
Nor skilful less, cheap conquest to ensure,
    Discord to breathe, and jealousy to sow,
To quell by boasting, and by bribes to lure ;
    While nought against them bring the unprac-
      tised foe,
Save hearts for Freedom's cause, and hands for
    Freedom's blow.

XLVIII.

Proudly they march—but, oh ! they march not
    forth
  By one hot field to crown a brief campaign,
As when their Eagles, sweeping through the
    North,
  Destroyed at every stoop an ancient reign !
Far other fate had Heaven decreed for Spain ;
  In vain the steel, in vain the torch was plied,
New Patriot armies started from the slain,
  High blazed the war, and long, and far, and
    wide,
And oft the God of Battles blest the righteous side.

XLIX.

Nor unatoned, where Freedom's foes prevail,
  Remained their savage waste. With blade and
    brand
By day the Invaders ravaged hill and dale,
  But, with the darkness, the Guerilla band
Came like night's tempest, and avenged the land,
  And claimed for blood the retribution due,
Probed the hard heart, and lopped the murd'rous
    hand ;
  And Dawn, when o'er the scene her beams she
    threw
'Midst ruins they had made, the spoilers' corpses
    knew.

L.

What minstrel verse may sing, or tongue may tell,
  Amid the visioned strife from sea to sea,
How oft the Patriot banners rose or fell,
  Still honoured in defeat as victory !
For that sad pageant of events to be
  Showed every form of fight by field and flood ;
Slaughter and Ruin, shouting forth their glee,
  Beheld, while riding on the tempest scud,
The waters choked with slain, the earth bedrenched
    with blood !

LI.

Then Zaragoza—blighted be the tongue
    That names thy name without the honour due !
For never hath the harp of Minstrel rung,
    Of faith so felly proved, so firmly true !
Mine, sap, and bomb thy shattered ruins knew,
    Each art of war's extremity had room,
Twice from thy half-sacked streets the foe withdrew,
    And when at length stern fate decreed thy doom,
They won not Zaragoza, but her children's bloody tomb.

LII.

Yet raise thy head, sad city !   Though in chains,
    Enthralled thou canst not be ! Arise, and claim
Reverence from every heart where Freedom reigns,
    For what thou worshippest ! — thy sainted dame,
She of the Column, honoured be her name
    By all, whate'er their creed, who honour love !
And like the sacred relics of the flame,
    That gave some martyr to the blessed above,
To every loyal heart may thy sad embers prove !

LIII.

Nor thine alone such wreck.   Gerona fair !
    Faithful to death thy heroes shall be sung,
Manning the towers, while o'er their heads the air
    Swart as the smoke from raging furnace hung ;
Now thicker darkening where the mine was sprung,
    Now briefly lightened by the cannon's flare,
Now arched with fire-sparks as the bomb was flung,
    And reddening now with conflagration's glare,
While by the fatal light the foes for storm prepare.

LIV.

While all around was danger, strife, and fear,
  While the earth shook, and darkened was the
    sky,
And wide Destruction stunned the listening ear,
  Appalled the heart, and stupefied the eye,—
Afar was heard that thrice-repeated cry,
  In which old Albion's heart and tongue unite,
Whene'er her soul is up, and pulse beats high,
  Whether it hail the wine-cup or the fight,
And bid each arm be strong, or bid each heart be
  light.

LV.

Don Roderick turned him as the shout grew
  loud—
  A varied scene the changeful vision showed,
For, where the ocean mingled with the cloud,
  A gallant navy stemmed the billows broad.
From mast and stern St. George's symbol flowed,
  Blent with the silver cross to Scotland dear;
Mottling the sea their landward barges rowed,
  And flashed the sun on bayonet, brand, and
    spear,
And the wild beach returned the seamen's jovial
  cheer.

LVI.

It was a dread, yet spirit-stirring sight!
  The billows foamed beneath a thousand oars,
Fast as they land the red-cross ranks unite,
  Legions on legions bright'ning all the shores.
Then banners rise, and cannon-signal roars,
  Then peals the warlike thunder of the drum,
Thrills the loud fife, the trumpet-flourish pours,
  And patriot hopes awake, and doubts are dumb,
For, bold in Freedom's cause, the bands of Ocean
  come!

LVII.

A various host they came—whose ranks display
    Each mode in which the warrior meets the fight,
The deep battalion locks its firm array,
    And meditates his aim the marksman light;
Far glance the light of sabres flashing bright
    Where mounted squadrons shake the echoing
        mead,
Lacks not artillery breathing flame and night,
    Nor the fleet ordnance whirled by rapid steed,
That rivals lightning's flash in ruin and in speed.

LVIII.

A various host —from kindred realms they came,
    Brethren in arms, but rivals in renown—
For yon fair bands shall merry England claim,
    And with their deeds of valour deck her crown.
Hers their bold port, and hers their martial frown,
    And hers their scorn of death in freedom's
        cause,
Their eyes of azure, and their locks of brown,
    And the blunt speech that bursts without a
        pause,
And free-born thoughts which league the Soldier
    with the Laws.

LIX.

And, oh! loved warriors of the Minstrel's land!
    Yonder your bonnets nod, your tartans wave!
The rugged form may mark the mountain band,
    And harsher features, and a mien more grave;
But ne'er in battlefield throbbed heart so brave
    As that which beats beneath the Scottish plaid;
And when the pibroch bids the battle rave,
    And level for the charge your arms are laid,
Where lives the desperate foe that for such onset
    stayed!

LX.

Hark! from yon stately ranks what laughter
      rings,
  Mingling wild mirth with war's stern minstrelsy,
His jest while each blithe comrade round him
      flings,
  And moves to death with military glee:
Boast, Erin, boast them! tameless, frank, and
      free,
  In kindness warm, and fierce in danger known,
Rough Nature's children, humorous as she:
  And HE, yon Chieftain—strike the proudest
      tone
Of thy bold harp, green Isle!—the Hero is thine
      own.

LXI.

Now on the scene Vimeira should be shown,
  On Talavera's fight should Roderick gaze,
And hear Corunna wail her battle won,
  And see Busaco's crest with lightning blaze:—
But shall fond fable mix with heroes' praise?
  Hath Fiction's stage for Truth's long triumphs
      room?
And dare her wild flowers mingle with the bays
  That claim a long eternity to bloom
Around the warrior's crest, and o'er the warrior's
      tomb!

LXII.

Or may I give adventurous Fancy scope,
  And stretch a bold hand to the awful veil
That hides futurity from anxious hope,
  Bidding beyond it scenes of glory hail,
And painting Europe rousing at the tale
  Of Spain's invaders from her confines hurled,
While kindling nations buckle on their mail,
  And Fame, with clarion-blast and wings un-
      furled,
To Freedom and Revenge awakes an injured World!

LXIII.

O vain, though anxious, is the glance I cast,
  Since Fate has marked futurity her own :
Yet Fate resigns to worth the glorious past,
  The deeds recorded, and the laurels won.
Then, though the Vault of Destiny be gone,
  King, Prelate, all the phantasms of my brain,
Melted away like mist-wreaths in the sun,
  Yet grant for faith, for valour, and for Spain,
One note of pride and fire, a Patriot's parting
    strain !

CONCLUSION.

I.

"Who shall command Estrella's mountain-tide
  Back to the source, when tempest-chafed, to
    hie ?
Who, when Gascogne's vexed gulf is raging wide,
  Shall hush it as a nurse her infant's cry ?
His magic power let such vain boaster try,
  And when the torrent shall his voice obey,
And Biscay's whirlwinds list his lullaby,
  Let him stand forth and bar mine eagles' way,
And they shall heed his voice, and at his bidding
    stay.

II.

" Else ne'er to stoop, till high on Lisbon's towers
  They close their wings, the symbol of our yoke,
And their own sea hath whelmed yon red-cross
    powers ! "
Thus, on the summit of Alverca's rock

To Marshal, Duke, and Peer, Gaul's Leader
   spoke.
  While downward on the land his legions press,
  Before them it was rich with vine and flock,
   And smiled like Eden in her summer dress ;—
Behind their wasteful march a reeking wilderness.

III.

And shall the boastful Chief maintain his word,
   Though Heaven hath heard the wailings of
    the land,
  Though Lusitania whet her vengeful sword,
   Though Britons arm and WELLINGTON com-
    mand !
No ! grim Busaco's iron ridge shall stand
   An adamantine barrier to his force ;
And from its base shall wheel his shattered band,
   As from the unshaken rock the torrent hoarse
Bears off its broken waves, and seeks a devious
    course.

IV.

Yet not because Alcoba's mountain-hawk
   Hath on his best and bravest made her food,
In numbers confident, yon Chief shall baulk
   His Lord's imperial thirst for spoil and blood :
For full in view the promised conquest stood,
   And Lisbon's matrons from their walls might
    sum
The myriads that had half the world subdued,
   And hear the distant thunders of the drum,
That bids the bands of France to storm and havoc
    come.

V.

Four moons have heard these thunders idly rolled,
   Have seen these wistful myriads eye their prey,
As famished wolves survey a guarded fold—
   But in the middle path a Lion lay !

At length they move—but not to battle-fray,
Nor blaze yon fires where meets the manly
fight ;
Beacons of infamy, they light the way
Where cowardice and cruelty unite
To damn with double shame their ignominious
flight.

VI.

O triumph for the Fiends of Lust and Wrath !
Ne'er to be told, yet ne'er to be forgot,
What wanton horrors marked their wreckful path !
The peasant butchered in his ruined cot,
The hoary priest even at the altar shot,
Childhood and age given o'er to sword and
flame,
Woman to infamy ;—no crime forgot,
By which inventive demons might proclaim
Immortal hate to man, and scorn of God's great
name !

VII.

The rudest sentinel, in Britain born,
With horror paused to view the havoc done,
Gave his poor crust to feed some wretch forlorn,
Wiped his stern eye, then fiercer grasped his
gun.
Nor with less zeal shall Britain's peaceful son
Exult the debt of sympathy to pay ;
Riches nor poverty the tax shall shun,
Nor prince nor peer, the wealthy nor the gay,
Nor the poor peasant's mite, nor bard's more worth-
less lay.

VIII.

But thou—unfoughten wilt thou yield to Fate,
Minion of Fortune, now miscalled in vain !
Can vantage-ground no confidence create,
Marcella's pass, nor Guarda's mountain-chain?

Vainglorious fugitive ! yet turn again !
　Behold, where, named by some prophetic Seer,
Flows Honour's Fountain,* as foredoomed the
　　stain
　From thy dishonoured name and arms to clear—
Fallen Child of Fortune, turn, redeem her favour
　　here !

IX.

Yet, ere thou turn'st, collect each distant aid ;
　Those chief that never heard the lion roar !
Within whose souls lives not a trace portrayed
　Of Talavera or Mondego's shore !
Marshal each band thou hast, and summon more ;
　Of war's fell stratagems exhaust the whole ;
Rank upon rank, squadron on squadron pour,
　Legion on legion on thy foeman roll,
And weary out his arm—thou canst not quell his
　　soul.

X.

O vainly gleams with steel Agueda's shore,
　Vainly thy squadrons hide Assuava's plain,
And front the flying thunders as they roar,
　With frantic charge and tenfold odds, in vain !
And what avails thee that, for CAMERON slain,
　Wild from his plaided ranks the yell was given—
Vengeance and grief gave mountain-range the
　　rein,
　And, at the bloody spear-point headlong
　　driven,
Thy Despot's giant guards fled like the rack of
　　heaven.

XI.

Go, baffled boaster ! teach thy haughty mood
　To plead at thine imperious master's throne,
Say, thou hast left his legions in their blood,
　Deceived his hopes, and frustrated thine own ;

---

* The literal translation of *Fuentes d'Honoro.*

Say, that thine utmost skill and valour shown,
By British skill and valour were outvied ;
Last say, thy conqueror was WELLINGTON !
And if he chafe, be his own fortune tried—
God and our cause to friend, the venture we'll
abide.

XII.

But you, ye heroes of that well-fought day,
How shall a bard, unknowing and unknown,
His meed to each victorious leader pay,
Or bind on every brow the laurels won?
Yet fain my harp would wake its boldest tone,
O'er the wide sea to hail CADOGAN brave ;
And he, perchance, the minstrel-note might own,
Mindful of meeting brief that Fortune gave
'Mid yon far western isles that hear the Atlantic
rave.

XIII.

Yes! hard the task, when Britons wield the
sword,
To give each Chief and every field its fame :
Hark! Albuera thunders BERESFORD,
And Red Barosa shouts for dauntless GRÆME !
O for a verse of tumult and of flame,
Bold as the bursting of their cannon sound,
To bid the world re-echo to their fame !
For never, upon gory battle-ground,
With conquest's well-bought wreath were braver
victors crowned !

XIV.

O who shall grudge him Albuera's bays,
Who brought a race regenerate to the field,
Roused them to emulate their fathers' praise,
Tempered their headlong rage, their courage
steeled,

And raised fair Lusitania's fallen shield,
    And gave new edge to Lusitania's sword,
    And taught her sons forgotten arms to wield—
      Shivered my harp, and burst its every chord,
If it forget thy worth, victorious BERESFORD !

XV.

Not on that bloody field of battle won,
    Though Gaul's proud legions rolled like mist
      away,
Was half his self-devoted valour shown,—
    He gaged but life on that illustrious day ;
But when he toiled those squadrons to array,
    Who fought like Britons in the bloody game,
Sharper than Polish pike or assagay,
    He braved the shafts of censure and of shame,
And, dearer far than life, he pledged a soldier's
      fame.

XVI.

Nor be his praise o'erpast who strove to hide
    Beneath the warrior's vest affection's wound,
Whose wish Heaven for his country's weal
      denied ;
    Danger and fate he sought, but glory found.
From clime to clime, where'er war's trumpets
      sound,
    The wanderer went ; yet Caledonia ! still
Thine was his thought in march and tented
      ground ;
    He dreamed 'mid Alpine cliffs of Athole's hill,
And heard in Ebro's roar his Lyndoch's lovely rill.

XVII.

O hero of a race renowned of old,
    Whose war-cry oft has waked the battle-swell,
Since first distinguished in the onset bold,
    Wild sounding when the Roman rampart fell !

By Wallace' side it rung the Southron's knell,
  Alderne, Kilsythe, and Tibber owned its fame,
Tummell's rude pass can of its terrors tell,
  But ne'er from prouder field arose the name
Than when wild Ronda learned the conquering
    shout of GRÆME!

XVIII.

But all too long, through seas unknown and
    dark,
  (With Spenser's parable I close my tale,)
By shoal and rock hath steered my venturous
    bark,
  And landward now I drive before the gale.
And now the blue and distant shore I hail,
  And nearer now I see the port expand,
And now I gladly furl my weary sail,
  And, as the prow light touches on the strand,
I strike my red-cross flag and bind my skiff to land.

The Field of Waterloo.

BY WALTER SCOTT.

—⁘—

I.

FAIR Brussels, thou art far behind,
Though, lingering on the morning wind,
   We yet may hear the hour
Pealed over orchard and canal,
With voice prolonged and measured fall,
   From proud St. Michael's tower ;
Thy wood, dark Soignies, holds us now,
Where the tall beeches' glossy bough
   For many a league around,
With birch and darksome oak between,
Spreads deep and far a pathless screen,
   Of tangled forest ground.
Stems planted close by stems defy
The adventurous foot—the curious eye
   For access seeks in vain ; ·
And the brown tapestry of leaves,
Strewed on the blighted ground, receives
Nor sun, nor air, nor rain.
No opening glade dawns on our way,
No streamlet, glancing to the ray,
   Our woodland path has crossed ;
And the straight causeway which we tread
Prolongs a line of dull arcade,
Unvarying through the unvaried shade
Until in distance lost.

II.

A brighter, livelier scene succeeds ;
In groups the scattering wood recedes,
Hedge-rows, and huts, and sunny meads,
    And corn-fields glance between ;
The peasant, at his labour blithe,
Plies the hooked staff and shortened scythe :—
    But when these ears were green,
Placed close within destruction's scope,
Full little was that rustic's hope
    Their ripening to have seen !
And, lo, a hamlet and its fane :—
Let not the gazer with disdain
    Their architecture view ;
For yonder rude ungraceful shrine,
And disproportioned spire, are thine,
    Immortal WATERLOO !

III.

Fear not the heat, though full and high
The sun has scorched the autumn sky,
And scarce a forest straggler now
To shade us spreads a greenwood bough ;
These fields have seen a hotter day
Than e'er was fired by sunny ray,
Yet one mile on—yon shattered hedge
Crests the soft hill whose long smooth ridge
    Looks on the field below,
And sinks so gently on the dale
That not the folds of Beauty's veil
    In easier curves can flow.
Brief space from thence, the ground again
Ascending slowly from the plain
    Forms an opposing screen,
Which, with its crest of upland ground,
Shuts the horizon all around.
    The softened vale between
Slopes smooth and fair for courser's tread ;
Not the most timid maid need dread

H

To give her snow-white palfrey head
   On that wide stubble-ground ;
Nor wood, nor tree, nor bush are there,
Her course to intercept or scare,
   Nor fosse nor fence are found,
Save where, from out her shattered bowers,
Rise Hougomont's dismantled towers.

IV.

Now, see'st thou aught in this lone scene
Can tell of that which late hath been ?—
   A stranger might reply,
" The bare extent of stubble-plain
Seems lately lightened of its grain ;
And yonder sable tracks remain
Marks of the peasant's ponderous wain,
   When harvest-home was nigh.
On these broad spots of trampled ground,
Perchance the rustics danced such round
   As Teniers loved to draw ;
And where the earth seems scorched by flame,
To dress the homely feast they came,
And toiled the kerchiefed village dame
   Around her fire of straw."

V.

So deem'st thou—so each mortal deems,
Of that which is from that which seems :—
   But other harvest here
Than that which peasant's scythe demands,
Was gathered in by sterner hands,
   With bayonet, blade, and spear.
No vulgar crop was theirs to reap,
No stinted harvest thin and cheap !
Heroes before each fatal sweep
   Fell thick as ripened grain ;
And ere the darkening of the day,
Piled high as autumn shocks, there lay
The ghastly harvest of the fray,
   The corpses of the slain.

VI.

Ay, look again—that line, so black
And trampled, marks the bivouac,
Yon deep-graved ruts the artillery's track,
    So often lost and won ;
And close beside, the hardened mud
Still shows where, fetlock-deep in blood,
The fierce dragoon, through battle's flood,
    Dashed the hot war-horse on.
These spots of excavation tell
The ravage of the bursting shell—
And feel'st thou not the tainted steam,
That reeks against the sultry beam,
    From yonder trenchéd mound ?
The pestilential fumes declare
That Carnage has replenished there
    Her garner-house profound.

VII.

Far other harvest-home and feast,
Than claims the boor from scythe released,
    On these scorched fields were known !
Death hovered o'er the maddening rout,
And, in the thrilling battle-shout,
Sent for the bloody banquet out
    A summons of his own.
Through rolling smoke the Demon's eye
Could well each destined guest espy,
Well could his ear in ecstasy
    Distinguish every tone
That filled the chorus of the fray—
From cannon-roar and trumpet-bray,
From charging squadrons' wild hurra,
From the wild clang that marked their way,—
    Down to the dying groan,
And the last sob of life's decay,
    When breath was all but flown.

VIII.

Feast on, stern foe of mortal life,
Feast on !—but think not that a strife,
With such promiscuous carnage rife,
　　Protracted space may last ;
The deadly tug of war at length
Must limits find in human strength,
　　And cease when these are past.
Vain hope !—that morn's o'erclouded sun
Heard the wild shout of fight begun
　　Ere he attained his height,
And through the war-smoke, volumed high,
Still peals that unremitted cry,
　　Though now he stoops to night.
For ten long hours of doubt and dread,
Fresh succours from the extended head
Of either hill the contest fed ;
　　Still down the slope they drew,
The charge of columns pauséd not,
Nor ceased the storm of shell and shot ;
　　For all that war could do
Of skill and force was proved that day,
And turned not yet the doubtful fray
　　On bloody Waterloo.

IX.

Pale Brussels ! then what thoughts were thine,
When ceaseless from the distant line
　　Continued thunders came !
Each burgher held his breath, to hear
These forerunners of havoc near,
　　Of rapine and of flame.
What ghastly sights were thine to meet,
When rolling through thy stately street,
The wounded showed their mangled plight
In token of the unfinished fight,
And from each anguish-laden wain
The blood-drops laid thy dust like rain !

How often in the distant drum
Heard'st thou the fell Invader come,
While Ruin, shouting to his band,
Shook high her torch and gory brand !—
Cheer thee, fair City !   From yon stand,
Impatient, still his outstretched hand
     Points to his prey in vain,
While maddening in his eager mood,
And all unwont to be withstood,
     He fires the fight again.

X.

" On ! On ! " was still his stern exclaim ;
" Confront the battery's jaws of flame !
     Rush on the levelled gun !
My steel-clad cuirassiers, advance !
Each Hulan forward with his lance,
My Guard—my Chosen—charge for France,
     France and Napoleon ! "
Loud answered their acclaiming shout,
Greeting the mandate which sent out
Their bravest and their best to dare
The fate their leader shunned to share.
But HE, his country's sword and shield,
Still in the battle-front revealed,
Where danger fiercest swept the field,
     Came like a beam of light,
In action prompt, in sentence brief—
" Soldiers, stand firm ! " exclaimed the Chief,
     " England shall tell the fight ! "

XI.

On came the whirlwind—like the last
But fiercest sweep of tempest-blast—
On came the whirlwind—steel-gleams broke
Like lightning through the rolling smoke ;
     The war was waked anew,
Three hundred cannon-mouths roared loud,
And from their throats, with flash and cloud,
     Their showers of iron threw.

Beneath their fire, in full career,
Rushed on the ponderous cuirassier,
The lancer couched his ruthless spear,
And hurrying as to havoc near,
    The cohorts' eagles flew.
In one dark torrent, broad and strong,
The advancing onset rolled along,
Forth harbingered by fierce acclaim,
That, from the shroud of smoke and flame,
Pealed wildly the imperial name.

XII.

But on the British heart were lost
The terrors of the charging host ;
For not an eye the storm that viewed
Changed its proud glance of fortitude,
Nor was one forward footstep stayed,
As dropped the dying and the dead.
Fast as their ranks the thunders tear,
Fast they renewed each serried square ;
And on the wounded and the slain
Closed their diminished files again,
Till from their line scarce spears'-lengths three,
Emerging from the smoke they see
Helmet, and plume, and panoply,—
    Then waked their fire at once !
Each musketeer's revolving knell,
As fast, as-regularly fell,
As when they practise to display
Their discipline on festal day.
    Then down went helm and lance,
Down were the eagle banners sent,
Down reeling steeds and riders went,
Corslets were pierced, and pennons rent ;
    And, to augment the fray,
Wheeled full against their staggering flanks,
The English horsemen's foaming ranks
    Forced their resistless way.
Then to the musket-knell succeeds
The clash of swords—the neigh of steeds—

As plies the smith his clanging trade,
Against the cuirass rang the blade ; ·
And while amid their close array
The well-served cannon rent their way,
And while amid their scattered band
Raged the fierce rider's bloody brand,
Recoiled in common rout and fear,
Lancer and guard and cuirassier,
Horsemen and foot,—a mingled host
Their leaders fall'n, their standards lost.

XIII.

Then, WELLINGTON ! thy piercing eye
This crisis caught of destiny—
   The British host had stood
That morn 'gainst charge of sword and lance
As their own ocean-rocks hold stance,
But when thy voice had said, "Advance!"
   They were their ocean's flood.—
O Thou, whose inauspicious aim
Hath wrought thy host this hour of shame,
Think'st thou thy broken bands will bide
The terrors of yon rushing tide?
Or will thy chosen brook to feel
The British shock of levelled steel,
   Or dost thou turn thine eye
Where coming squadrons gleam afar,
And fresher thunders wake the war,
   And other standards fly?—
Think not that in yon columns, file
Thy conquering troops from distant Dyle—
   Is Blucher yet unknown?
Or dwells not in thy memory still
(Heard frequent in thine hour of ill),
What notes of hate and vengeance thrill
   In Prussia's trumpet-tone ?—
What yet remains?—shall it be thine
To head the relics of thy line
   In one dread effort more?—

The Roman lore thy leisure loved,
And thou canst tell what fortune proved
    That Chieftain, who, of yore,
Ambition's dizzy paths essayed
And with the gladiators' aid
    For empire enterprised—
He stood the cast his rashness played,
Left not the victims he had made,
Dug his red grave with his own blade,
And on the field he lost was laid,
    Abhorred—but not despised.

XIV.

But if revolves thy fainter thought
On safety—howsoever bought,—
Then turn thy fearful rein and ride,
Though twice ten thousand men have died
    On this eventful day
To gild the military fame
Which thou, for life, in traffic tame
    Wilt barter thus away.
Shall future ages tell this tale
Of inconsistence faint and frail?
And art thou He of Lodi's bridge,
Marengo's field, and Wagram's ridge!
    Or is thy soul like mountain-tide,
That, swelled by winter storm and shower,
Rolls down in turbulence of power,
    A torrent fierce and wide;
Reft of these aids, a rill obscure,
Shrinking unnoticed, mean and poor,
    Whose channel shows displayed
The wrecks of its impetuous course,
But not one symptom of the force
    By which these wrecks were made!

XV.

Spur on thy way!—since now thine ear
Has brooked thy veterans' wish to hear,
    Who, as thy flight they eyed

Exclaimed,—while tears of anguish came,
Wrung forth by pride, and rage, and shame,
    "O that he had but died ! "
But yet, to sum this hour of ill,
Look, ere thou leav'st the fatal hill,
        Back on yon broken ranks—
Upon whose wild confusion gleams
The moon, as on the troubled streams
        When rivers break their banks,
And, to the ruined peasant's eye,
Objects half seen roll swiftly by,
        Down the dread current hurled—
So mingle banner, wain, and gun,
Where the tumultuous flight rolls on
Of warriors, who, when morn begun,
        Defied a banded world.

XVI.

List—frequent to the hurrying rout,
The stern pursuers' vengeful shout
Tells, that upon their broken rear
Rages the Prussian's bloody spear.
        So fell a shriek was none,
When Beresina's icy flood
Reddened and thawed with flame and blood,
And, pressing on thy desperate way,
Raised oft and long their wild hurra,
        The children of the Don.
Thine ear no yell of horror cleft
So ominous, when, all bereft
Of aid, the valiant Polack left—
Ay, left by thee—found soldier's grave
In Leipsic's corpse-encumbered wave.
Fate, in those various perils past,
Reserved thee still some future cast ;
On the dread die thou now hast thrown
Hangs not a single field alone,
Nor one campaign—thy martial fame,
Thy empire, dynasty, and name
        Have felt the final stroke ;

H 2

And now, o'er thy devoted head
The last stern vial's wrath is shed,
　　The last dread seal is broke.

XVII.

Since live thou wilt—refuse not now
Before these demagogues to bow,
Late objects of thy scorn and hate,
Who shall thy once imperial fate
Make wordy theme of vain debate.—
Or shall we say, thou stoop'st less low
In seeking refuge from the foe,
Against whose heart, in prosperous life,
Thine hand hath ever held the knife?
　　Such homage hath been paid
By Roman and by Grecian voice,
And there were honour in the choice,
　　If it were freely made.
Then safely come—in one so low,—
So lost,—we cannot own a foe;
Though dear experience bid us end,
In thee we ne'er can hail a friend.—
Come, howsoe'er—but do not hide
Close in thy heart that germ of pride,
Erewhile, by gifted bard espied,
　　That "yet imperial hope;"
Think not that for a fresh rebound,
To raise ambition from the ground,
　　We yield thee means or scope.
In safety come—but ne'er again
Hold type of independent reign;
　　No islet calls thee lord,
We leave thee no confederate band,
No symbol of thy lost command,
To be a dagger in the hand
　　From which we wrenched the sword.

XVIII.

Yet, even in yon sequestered spot,
May worthier conquest be thy lot
　　Than yet thy life has known;

Conquest, unbought by blood or harm,
That needs nor foreign aid nor arm,
   A triumph all thine own.
Such waits thee when thou shalt control
Those passions wild, that stubborn soul,
   That marred thy prosperous scene :—
Hear this—from no unmovéd heart,
Which sighs, comparing what THOU ART
   With what thou MIGHT'ST HAVE BEEN !

XIX.

Thou, too, whose deeds of fame renewed
Bankrupt a nation's gratitude,
To thine own noble heart must owe
More than the meed she can bestow.
For not a people's just acclaim,
Not the full hail of Europe's fame,
Thy Prince's smiles, the State's decree,
The ducal rank, the gartered knee,
Not these such pure delight afford
As that, when hanging up thy sword,
Well may'st thou think, " This honest steel
Was ever drawn for public weal ;
And, such was rightful Heaven's decree,
Ne'er sheathed unless with victory ! "

XX.

Look forth, once more, with softened heart,
Ere from the field of fame we part ;
Triumph and Sorrow border near,
And joy oft melts into a tear.
Alas ! what links of love that morn
Has War's rude hand asunder torn !
For ne'er was field so sternly fought,
And ne'er was conquest dearer bought,
Here piled in common slaughter sleep
Those whom affection long shall weep :
Here rests the sire, that ne'er shall strain
His orphans to his heart again ;

The son, whom, on his native shore,
The parent's voice shall bless no more ;
The bridegroom, who has hardly pressed
His blushing consort to his breast ;
The husband, whom through many a year
Long love and mutual faith endear.
Thou canst not name one tender tie,
But here dissolved its relics lie!
Oh ! when thou see'st some mourner's veil
Shroud her thin form and visage pale,
Or mark'st the Matron's bursting tears
Stream when the stricken drum she hears ;
Or see'st how manlier grief, suppressed,
Is labouring in a father's breast,—
With no inquiry vain pursue
The cause, but think on Waterloo !

XXI.

Period of honour as of woes,
What bright careers 'twas thine to close !—
Marked on thy roll of blood what names
To Britain's memory, and to Fame's,
Laid there their last immortal claims !
Thou saw'st in seas of gore expire
Redoubted PICTON's soul of fire—
Saw'st in the mingled carnage lie
All that of PONSONBY could die—
DE LANCEY change Love's bridal-wreath
For laurels from the hand of Death—
Saw'st gallant MILLER's failing eye
Still bent where Albion's banners fly,
And CAMERON, in the shock of steel,
Die like the offspring of Lochiel ;
And generous GORDON, 'mid the strife,
Fall while he watched his leader's life.—
Ah ! though her guardian angel's shield
Fenced Britain's hero through the field,
Fate not the less her power made known,
Through his friends' hearts to pierce his own !

XXII.

Forgive, brave Dead, the imperfect lay!
Who may your names, your numbers, say?
What high-strung harp, what lofty line,
To each the dear-earned praise assign,
From high-born chiefs of martial fame
To the poor soldier's lowlier name?
Lightly ye rose that dawning day,
From your cold couch of swamp and clay,
To fill, before the sun was low,
The bed that morning cannot know.—
Oft may the tear the green sod steep,
And sacred be the heroes' sleep,
　　Till time shall cease to run;
And ne'er beside their noble grave,
May Briton pass and fail to crave
A blessing on the fallen brave
　　Who fought with Wellington!

XXIII.

Farewell, sad Field! whose blighted face
Wears desolation's withering trace;
Long shall my memory retain
Thy shattered huts and trampled grain,
With every mark of martial wrong,
That scathe thy towers, fair Hougomont!
Yet though thy garden's green arcade
The marksman's fatal post was made,
Though on thy shattered beeches fell
The blended rage of shot and shell,
Though from thy blackened portals torn,
Their fall thy blighted fruit-trees mourn,
Has not such havoc bought a name
Immortal in the rolls of fame?
Yes—Agincourt may be forgot,
And Cressy be an unknown spot,
　　And Blenheim's name be new;
But still in story and in song,
For many an age remembered long,
Shall live the towers of Hougomont
　　And Field of Waterloo!

CONCLUSION.

STERN tide of human Time! that know'st not
    rest,
But, sweeping from the cradle to the tomb,
Bear'st ever downward on thy dusky breast
Successive generations to their doom ;
While thy capacious stream has equal room
For the gay bark where Pleasure's steamers
    sport,
And for the prison-ship of guilt and gloom,
The fisher-skiff, and barge that bears a court,
Still wafting onward all to one dark silent port ;—

Stern tide of Time ! through what mysterious
    change
Of hope and fear have our frail barks been
    driven !
For ne'er, before, vicissitude so strange
Was to one race of Adam's offspring given.
And sure such varied change of sea and heaven,
Such unexpected bursts of joy and woe,
Such fearful strife as that where we have striven,
Succeeding ages ne'er again shall know,
Until the awful term when Thou shalt cease to
    flow.

Well hast thou stood, my Country !—the brave
    fight
Hast well maintained through good report and
    ill ;
In thy just cause and in thy native might,
And in Heaven's grace and justice constant
    still ;

Whether the banded prowess, strength, and skill
Of half the world against thee stood arrayed,
Or when, with better views and freer will,
Beside thee Europe's noblest drew the blade,
Each emulous in arms the Ocean Queen to aid.

Well art thou now repaid—though slowly rose,
And struggled long with mists thy blaze of fame,
While likè the dawn that in the orient glows
On the broad wave its earlier lustre came;
Then eastern Egypt saw the growing flame,
And Maida's myrtles gleamed beneath its ray,
Where first the soldier, stung with generous
    shame,
Rivalled the heroes of the watery way,
And washed in foemen's gore unjust reproach away.

Now, Island Empress, wave thy crest on high,
And bid the banner of thy Patron flow,
Gallant Saint George, the flower of Chivalry,
For thou hast faced, like him, a dragon foe,
And rescued innocence from overthrow,
And trampled down, like him, tyrannic might,
And to the gazing world may'st proudly show
The chosen emblem of thy sainted Knight,
Who quelled devouring pride and vindicated right.

Yet 'mid the confidence of just renown,
Renown dear-bought, but dearest thus acquired,
Write, Britain, write the moral lesson down:
'Tis not alone the heart with valour fired,
The discipline so dreaded and admired,
In many a field of bloody conquest known,
—Such may by fame be lured, by gold be hired:
'Tis constancy in the good cause alone
Best justifies the meed thy valiant sons have won.

The Dance of Death.

[1815.]

—❧—

I.

NIGHT and morning were at meeting
    Over Waterloo ;
Cocks had sung their earliest greeting ;
    Faint and low they crew,
For no paly beam yet shone
On the heights of Mount Saint John ;
Tempest-clouds prolonged the sway
Of timeless darkness over day ;
Whirlwind, thunder-clap, and shower
Marked it a predestined hour.
Broad and frequent through the night
Flashed the sheets of levin-light :
Muskets, glancing lightnings back,
Showed the dreary bivouac
    Where the soldier lay,
Chill and stiff, and drenched with rain,
Wishing dawn of morn again,
    Though death should come with day.

II.

'Tis at such a tide and hour
Wizard, witch, and fiend have power,
And ghastly forms through mist and shower
    Gleam on the gifted ken ;
And then the affrighted prophet's ear
Drinks whispers strange of fate and fear
Presaging death and ruin near
    Among the sons of men ;—
184

Apart from Albyn's war-array,
'Twas then grey Allan sleepless lay ;
Grey Allan, who, for many a day,
    Had followed stout and stern,
Where, through battle's rout and reel,
Storm of shot and edge of steel,
Led the grandson of Lochiel,
    Valiant Fassiefern.
Through steel and shot he leads no more,
Low laid 'mid friends' and foemen's gore—
But long his native lake's wild shore,
And Sunart rough, and high Ardgower,
    And Morven long shall tell,
And proud Bennevis hear with awe
How, upon bloody Quatre-Bras,
Brave Cameron heard the wild hurra
    Of conquest as he fell.

III.

Lone on the outskirts of the host,
The weary sentinel held post,
And heard, through darkness far aloof,
The frequent clang of courser's hoof,
Where held the cloaked patrol their course,
And spurred 'gainst storm the swerving horse ;
But there are sounds in Allan's ear,
Patrol nor sentinel may hear,
And sights before his eye aghast
Invisible to them have passed,
    When down the destined plain,
'Twixt Britain and the bands of France,
Wild as marsh-borne meteor's glance,
Strange phantoms wheeled a revel dance,
    And doomed the future slain.—
Such forms were seen, such sounds were heard,
When Scotland's James his march prepared
    For Flodden's fatal plain ;
Such, when he drew his ruthless sword,
As Choosers of the Slain, adored
    The yet unchristened Dane.

An indistinct and phantom band,
They wheeled their ring-dance hand in hand,
　　With gestures wild and dread ;
The Seer, who watched them ride the storm,
Saw through their faint and shadowy form
　　The lightning's flash more red ;
And still their ghastly roundelay
Was of the coming battle-fray,
　　And of the destined dead.

IV.

SONG.

Wheel the wild dance
While lightnings glance,
　　And thunders rattle loud,
And call the brave
To bloody grave,
　　To sleep without a shroud.

Our airy feet,
So light and fleet,
　　They do not bend the rye
That sinks its head when whirlwinds rave,
And swells again in eddying wave,
　　As each wild gust blows by ;
But still the corn,
At dawn of morn,
　　Our fatal steps that bore,
At eve lies waste,
A trampled paste
　　Of blackening mud and gore.
Wheel the wild dance
While lightnings glance,
　　And thunders rattle loud,
And call the brave
To bloody grave,
　　To sleep without a shroud.

Wheel the wild dance !
Brave sons of France,
  For you our ring makes room ;
Make space full wide
For martial pride,
  For banner, spear, and plume.
Approach, draw near,
Proud cuirassier !
  Room for the men of steel !
Through crest and plate
The broadsword's weight
  Both head and heart shall feel.

VI.

Wheel the wild dance
While lightnings glance,
  And thunders rattle loud,
And call the brave
To bloody grave,
  To sleep without a shroud.

Sons of the spear !
You feel us near
  In many a ghastly dream ;
With fancy's eye
Our forms you spy,
  And hear our fatal scream.
With clearer sight
Ere falls the night,
  Just when to weal or woe
Your disembodied souls take flight
On trembling wing—each startled sprite
  Our choir of death shall know.

VII.

Wheel the wild dance
While lightnings glance,
  And thunders rattle loud,

And call the brave
To bloody grave,
  To sleep without a shroud.

Burst, ye clouds, in tempest showers,
Redder rain shall soon be ours—
  See the east grows wan—
Yield we place to sterner game,
Ere deadlier bolts and direr flame
Shall the welkin's thunders shame,
Elemental rage is tame
  To the wrath of man.

VIII.

At morn, grey Allan's mates with awe
Heard of the visioned sights he saw,
  The legend heard him say ;
But the Seer's gifted eye was dim,
Deafened his ear, and stark his limb,
  Ere closed that bloody day.
He sleeps far from his Highland heath,
But often of the Dance of Death
His comrades tell the tale
On picquet-post, when ebbs the night,
And waning watch-fires glow less bright,
  And dawn is glimmering pale.

Romance of Dunois.

FROM THE FRENCH.

[1815.]

—ᴐᴣ᷏ᴏ-

[The original of this little Romance makes part of
a manuscript collection of French Songs, probably
compiled by some young officer, which was found
on the field of Waterloo, so much stained with clay
and with blood as sufficiently to indicate what had
been the fate of its late owner. The song is popu-
lar in France, and is rather a good specimen of
the style of composition to which it belongs. The
translation is strictly literal.]

It was Dunois, the young and brave, was bound
    for Palestine,
But first he made his orisons before Saint Mary's
    shrine :
" And grant, immortal Queen of Heaven," was still
    the Soldier's prayer,
" That I may prove the bravest knight, and love
    the fairest fair."

His oath of honour on the shrine he graved it with
    his sword,
And followed to the Holy Land the banner of his
    Lord ;
Where, faithful to his noble vow, his war-cry filled
    the air,
" Be honoured aye the bravest knight, beloved the
    fairest fair."

They owed the conquest to his arm, and then his
    Liege-Lord said,
" The heart that has for honour beat by bliss must
    be repaid.—
My daughter Isabel and thou shall be a wedded
    pair,
For thou art bravest of the brave, she fairest of the
    fair."

And then they bound the holy knot before Saint
    Mary's shrine,
That makes a paradise on earth, if hearts and
    hands combine;
And every lord and lady bright that were in chapel
    there
Cried, " Honoured be the bravest knight, beloved
    the fairest fair!"

THE TROUBADOUR.

FROM THE SAME COLLECTION.

[1815.]

GLOWING with love, on fire for fame
    A Troubadour that hated sorrow
Beneath his lady's window came,
    And thus he sung his last good-morrow:
" My arm it is my country's right,
    My heart is in my true-love's bower;
Gaily for love and fame to fight
    Befits the gallant Troubadour."

And while he marched with helm on head
    And harp in hand, the descant rung,
As faithful to his favourite maid,
    The minstrel-burden still he sung:
" My arm it is my country's right,
    My heart is in my lady's bower;
Resolved for love and fame to fight
    I come, a gallant Troubadour."

Even when the battle-roar was deep,
 With dauntless heart he hewed his way,
'Mid splintering lance and falchion-sweep,
 And still was heard his warrior-lay :
" My life it is my country's right,
 My heart is in my lady's bower ;
For love to die, for fame to fight,
 Becomes the valiant Troubadour."

Alas ! upon the bloody field
 He fell beneath the foeman's glaive,
But still reclining on his shield,
 Expiring sung the exulting stave :—
" My life it is my country's right,
 My heart is in my lady's bower ;
For love and fame to fall in fight
 Becomes the valiant Troubadour."

PIBROCH OF DONALD DHU.

[This is a very ancient pibroch belonging to Clan
MacDonald. The words of the set, theme, or
melody, to which the pipe variations are applied,
run thus in Gaelic :—

Piobaireachd Dhonuil Dhuidh, piobaireachd Dhonuil ;
Piobaireachd Dhonuil Dhuidh, piobaireachd Dhonuil ;
Piobaireachd Dhonuil Dhuidh, piobaireachd Dhonuil ;
Piob agus bratach air faiche Inverlochi.
The pipe-summons of Donald the Black,
The pipe-summons of Donald the Black,
The war-pipe and the pennon are on the gathering-place
 at Inverlochy.]

PIBROCH of Donuil Dhu,
 Pibroch of Donuil,
Wake thy wild voice anew,
 Summon Clan Conuil.
Come away, come away,
 Hark to the summons !

Come in your war array,
  Gentles and commons.

Come from deep glen, and
  From mountain so rocky,
The war-pipe and pennon
  Are at Inverlochy.
Come every hill-plaid, and
  True heart that wears one,
Come every steel blade, and
  Strong hand that bears one.

Leave untended the herd,
  The flock without shelter;
Leave the corpse uninterr'd,
  The bride at the altar;
Leave the deer, leave the steer,
  Leave nets and barges:
Come with your fighting gear,
  Broadswords and targes.

Come as the winds come, when
  Forests are rended;
Come as the waves come, when
  Navies are stranded:
Faster come, faster come,
  Faster and faster,
Chief, vassal, page and groom,
  Tenant and master.

Fast they come, fast they come;
  See how they gather!
Wide waves the eagle plume,
  Blended with heather.
Cast your plaids, draw your blades,
  Forward each man set!
Pibroch of Donuil Dhu,
  Knell for the onset!

Printed by BALLANTYNE, HANSON & CO.
Edinburgh and London